The Black Scarface Series Presents:

BLACK GOTTI

A Novel By

JIMMY DASAINT

BLACK GOTTI

All Rights Reserved © 2017 DASAINT ENTERTAINMENT LLC.

No part of this book may be reproduced, distributed, or transmitted in any form or by any means, or stored in a database or retrieval system, without written permission from the publisher.

Sale of this book without the front cover may be unauthorized. If this book is without a cover, it may have been reported to the publisher as "unsold or destroyed" and neither the author (s) nor publisher may have received payment for it.

This work is a work of fiction. Any resemblance to real people, living or dead, actual events, establishments, or locales is intended to give the fiction a sense of reality and authenticity. Other names, characters, places, and incidents are either product of the authors' imagination or used fictitiously. Those fictionalized events and incidents that involve real persons did not occur and may be set in the future.

Published by DASAINT ENTERTAINMENT
Po Box 97 Bala Cynwyd, PA 19004
Website: www.dasaintentertainment.com

"Teach us to number our days that we may gain a heart of wisdom."

-Psalm 90:12

"There are no limits. There are only plateaus, and you must not stay there, you must go beyond them."

-Bruce Lee

Chapter 1
9:52 pm
Philadelphia, PA

Inside a lavish City Line apartment, two young men sat at a round wooden table breaking down three kilograms of pure Colombian cocaine. 27-year-old Simon Carter, also known on the streets of Philly as Black Gotti and his best friend Marvin Washington had been crime partners in the lucrative Philly drug trade for the past three years. Simon, who stood around 5' 10', had a dark brown complexion and a stocky build like an NFL fullback. His dark, curly hair came from his father's Italian heritage, while the rest of his features came from his Black mother. His signature dark black mole was right under his piercing hazel eyes, accentuating his model-like looks.

    Marvin had been his right-hand man since they were first introduced by a mutual friend at the Juvenile Detention Center. Standing at just 5' 8", he had the heart of a giant and was one of the most violent men walking the Philly streets. At just 25 years of age, Marvin had over six murders under his belt. He was known as a cold-blooded killer, respected by few and feared by many.

    On the table was a box of Ziplock bags, a digital scale and a loaded .40 caliber pistol. The two men each had on rubber surgical gloves, placing ounces of cocaine at a time inside the Ziplock bags. Gotti and Marvin were wholesale drug distributors who both worked for the King Cartel. Before they started working for King, they were two mid-level drug dealers buying cocaine from King's older, notorious cousin Scarface.

"Did you put the money in the stash?" Gotti asked. "Yup! All of it. Every single dime," Marvin replied. "Cool. We should have a little over $500 grand stacked," Gotti said with a smile.

Parked right outside in a stolen Ford Taurus four masked men had been waiting around for the past hour. For the past few weeks, they had been secretly watching and plotting Gotti's and Marvin's every move. And today was the day to finally make their move. With the dark black sky hiding their criminal intentions, they tightly clutched 9 mm's and calmly stepped out of the car.

"You got the key card?" one of the men asked. "I got it, we good." The four men entered the quiet apartment building and walked down the empty hall. The building was mostly housed by older, rich senior citizens and retired police, firefighters and government workers.

Approaching apartment 115 the four masked men stood around calmly. After a long deep breath, one of the men raised his gun then nodded his head. With that signal, the four masked men kicked in the door and burst into the apartment with pistols aiming.

"Get the fuck down on the floor!" one of the men yelled. Gotti and Marvin were completely startled and quickly laid down on the floor without saying a word. Both men angrily watched as two of the men stood over them aiming guns at their heads while the other two put the kilos of cocaine and the loaded .40 caliber inside a backpack.

"Where's the money?" one of the men asked. "Ain't no money!" Gotti replied. "We just copped up."

"He lying," another man said. "Let's check the crib." "No, ain't no time for that, we got what we wanted. Let's go before the cops get here."

In less than five minutes, the four men had robbed and gotten away with three kilos, a street value of $100,000, and a brand new pistol. All without firing a single shot. After the men ran out of the apartment, Marvin and Gotti grabbed their guns from underneath their shirts and ran after the culprits. When they reached the front lobby, they saw a dark Ford Taurus speeding off down the street.

"Someone set us up!!" Marvin shouted. Gotti stood there in total silence, with a look of pure anger plastered on his face. Someone has to die for this, he thought to himself. And neither man would rest until they found out who.

Chapter 2

After the four masked men had gotten away with three kilos and a new gun, Gotti and Marvin quickly ran back into the apartment. After packing up their valuables, they cleaned up the entire spot and rushed out the door, never to return. It was one of the few stash spots they had located throughout Philly. Before leaving Marvin had taken the surveillance video from the recorder. If they hadn't been too busy packing up the cocaine they both would have seen the masked men before they burst through the front door. Each man was determined to get to the bottom of this.

The three kilo lost was a major hit and getting it back was going to be almost impossible. After placing their belongings in the trunk of Gotti's black Mercedes Benz they both got inside and the car sped off in the darkness of the cold Philly night.

...

Nookie's Afterhours Bar and Night Club was one of the most popular Afterhours spots in West Philly. It was located in a large, three-story building on 42nd Street. Nookie's was the late night spot for pimps, hookers, hustlers, gamblers, and drug dealers that had been working the streets all day. It had a huge built in bar, with every bottle of liquor, wine, and vodka you could name on the shelves. It also had two large poker tables, a craps table, and two large all black pool tables.

The owner of the spot was a 62-year-old O-G named Big Nook, a 300 lb former member of the Philly Black Mafia from the 70's and early 80's. Big Nook stood at 6' 6" tall with a dark black complexion, and he had the huge body of a professional wrestler. Even in his early 60's Big Nook was still a feared and well-respected man. His pride and joy was his beautiful daughter Tori. She was the apple of his eye and his only weakness. Tori helped manage the club and was one of the three female bartenders. Tori was a 22-year-old, petite, light skinned woman with a beautiful face. Her piercing green eyes accentuated her gorgeous looks. She was a Temple student by day and a bartender by night. Tori's goal was to become an accountant one day. At the rate she was going, it would happen much sooner than later.

Inside Nookie's the club was packed to full capacity. The DJ was playing all the latest rap and R&B songs, getting the boisterous crowd more into the mood. The two large bouncers had to politely remove a few drunks from the premises.

At a small table in the back, Big Nook and his spoiled son Troy was having a private conversation. Troy was almost a spitting image of his father, just 100 pounds lighter. From a distance, Tori watched as her father and brother seemed to be having a heated, intense conversation. Most people were used to seeing the two men verbally attacking each other, but Tori could see that this time it was much more to it.

After serving a customer, Tori watched as her brother and father stood up from the table and walked out the back door. Twenty minutes later, Big Nook walked back inside alone.

"Is everything okay Daddy?" Big Nook placed his large arms around his daughter's shoulders and said, "Yes, baby girl everything is fine. Your damn brother pisses me off sometimes. He can't never get anything I tell him to do right the first time."

"Well give him another chance Dad. Troy loves you and it's nothing that he wouldn't do to prove it to you." "Enough about Troy, let's go have a drink and talk about what's going on with you baby girl." "So, can we finally have a real talk about my boyfriend?" She asked.

"No. Anything but him," Big Nook replied in a serious voice. "Okay Daddy, but give him a fair chance and one day he will grow on you." "Maybe one day, just not today." He said.

Chapter 3
26th & Huntingdon
North Philly

The four masked men jumped out of a stolen minivan and rushed towards a house on the corner. With pistols in hand, they kicked in the front door. The group of men inside were told to lay down on the floor with their hands behind their backs. As two of the armed men stood over them, the other two men ran through the house searching for money and drugs.

"Bingo," one of the men said, after looking through an upstairs closet and finding a Nike sports bag filled with four kilos of cocaine and over $200,000 in cash. One of the men who was tied up and lying on the floor was named Gee. As he laid there, he took mental notes of both individuals. The first thing he noticed was that both men were wearing the latest Jordan sneakers. He made a mental note of it. When the other two men ran down the stairs all four of them rushed back out the front door.

After hearing the sounds of a speeding van drive off the five men on the floor began to untie themselves. They had just taken a major loss, and neither of them could believe what had just happened. They were a group of drug dealers known as the Bottom Boyz and taking money and robbing drug dealers was their thing, not the other way around.

"Somebody set us the fuck up!" Gee shouted. "They got the Nike bag full of the work and cash!"

One of the men walked up to Gee and said, "So are you going to call King and tell him what happened?" Gee just stood there shaking his head in total disbelief. It was the first time he had ever been robbed. Gee walked over to the broken down front door and noticed a large Jordan footprint on it. He was almost positive that the print was a size 11 because that was his own shoe size. Then he looked back at his crew and said, "Where's my cell phone? I'm calling King right now."

After one of the men had retrieved Gee's cell phone, he stepped out on the porch and called his cousin King. King was the biggest drug dealer in the entire tri-state area.

The Mercedes Benz pulled up and parked in front of a small row house on 18th & Tioga Street. Gotti and Marvin quickly jumped out of the car and rushed into the house. Inside waiting was their good friend Roscoe. Roscoe was a 23-year-old short, chubby light-skinned guy with a face full of freckles. He was also a computer and tech geek that mostly stayed inside the house on his computers hacking or playing video games. When it came to the internet or gathering crucial information, there was nothing or no one that Roscoe couldn't find or dig up dirt on. All day long Roscoe would pursue his personal passion of being one of the best computer hackers and internet scammers around. He was a loner and a weirdo, and that's how he liked it.

"What's up fellas? What's the emergency?" Roscoe asked as he rolled his chair over to his computer desk. Marvin passed Roscoe a small disk and said, "We just got robbed and this is the surveillance disc that had been recording the whole time. We want you to check it out and find out everything that you can on the niggas that set us up! Take your time and see what you can come up with and call me after you are done."

"No problem fellas, I'm on it," Roscoe said, as he inserted the disc into his laptop. Gotti reached into his pocket and pulled out a stack of hundred dollar bills. He pulled out five of them and passed it to Roscoe.

"Damn y'all must really want these guys…or girls…or aliens," Roscoe said with a weird smile on his face. "Just find out what you can!" Gotti said in a serious tone. Seeing how serious the situation was Roscoe quickly fixed his face. After shaking hands, he watched as Gotti and Marvin rushed back out the door. "Okay, it's work time," he said to himself.

Chapter 4
A few hours later
Wynnewood. PA

Wynnewood, Pennsylvania is a quiet suburban town west of Philadelphia. Most of the residents that live there are professionals, lawyers, doctors, architects and professional athletes. Nestled in a lavish condominium, Gotti sat back on the soft leather sofa in deep thought. Since the robbery, he had been very agitated. The thought of being tied up and robbed by four men was eating him up inside. Whoever was responsible would die for their actions. He wouldn't rest until he was standing over their graves pissing on their tombstones. He was a prideful man, and today his pride had taken a major hit.

As he sat there zoned out the sound of a turning doorknob quickly snapped him out of his trance. Then walked in his beautiful girlfriend. "What's wrong honey, I came as soon as you texted me," Tori said, as she took off her coat and rushed over to his side. She placed her arms around him and they passionately kissed.

"Is everything okay Daddy?" Tori could tell that something was deeply troubling Gotti. She had never seen a more serious expression on his face. "No! Somebody set me and Marvin the fuck up! They got us for three bricks and a pistol!"

Tori was in complete shock. No one robbed Gotti. His name was feared and respected all throughout

Philly, Camden, Delaware, Chester, Atlantic City and beyond. Tori grabbed his hands and said, "Baby, don't let this stress you out. You're a boss! You have over $500,000 put away. Don't let money make and control you, boss up and be the nigga I fell in love with."

Gotti smiled and just shook his head. This is why he loved his girlfriend Tori; she was a rider and his rock when he needed an ear to listen to and a shoulder to lean on. "Now take off them Timbs and clothes and take me back into our bedroom and take all your stress out on this pink, wet pussy!" Tori said, before standing up and walking towards the bedroom.

The Next Day, West Philly

Two Philadelphia police cars pulled up in the back of Nookie's Afterhours Club. The four officers exited the vehicles and approached the door. Big Nook walked out the door before the cops could enter. "Wassup fellas? I paid y'all off last week," he said.

"You good Big Nook, we need to speak to your son Troy," one of the cops said. "Why, wassup? What did he do now?" Big Nook asked concernedly.

"We just need to talk to him. The streets keep whispering his name. Robberies, drug dealing, murders, the list is endless," an officer replied. Big Nook crossed his arms and smiled.

"If y'all don't have an arrest warrant then y'all just wasting your time. Tell all your rats and informants to go to hell! My boy ain't do shit!"

Big Nook watched as one cop stuck his head out of the window and said, "Just tell Troy that we need to see him. And Big Nook, everything ain't always as it seems."

The two police cars backed out and pulled off. As soon as they were gone Big Nook pulled out his cell phone and called Troy. "Wassup Pop?" he answered. "The cops came by the club looking for your ass! What's going on Troy? What did your ass do this time?"

"Pop calm down. Everything is cool. I'm good; you know how these Philly cops are. They just trying to scare me. It's the third time the cops came looking for me and not once have I been locked up. Fuck the cops, the Feds and anybody else that's mentioning my name. I ain't do shit!"

Big Nook listened as his son vented out his frustrations. He understood what he was going through. Being a former member of Philly Black Mafia, he knew exactly how the cops like to play people. It was a game they played all too well.

"Just be careful Tory. I don't trust no cop, especially Philly cops!" "I'm good Pops. I will see you at the club later tonight," Troy said before ending the call. With that said Big Nook casually walked back into his popular, money-making establishment.

The Federal Building

"We have to do something about these drug dealers!" James Hightower vented out to his assistant Roy Carter. James Hightower was the top Federal Prosecutor for the Eastern District of Pennsylvania. "Don't worry sir. We will get them all. We have some major informants on the streets that are out gathering all the information we will need to do a major FBI and DEA sweep in the coming months, "Roy said with enthusiasm.

Roy Carter was the prosecutor's personal assistant. After working in the FBI for 14 years, he had been hired by James Hightower because of his legal background and his spotless record at the Bureau.

"Roy, when you get a chance I need you to set up a meeting with Candice Shaw. My bosses in Washington have been down my ass about all the murders, drugs and corruption in Philadelphia. We have to pull all of our resources and start taking these lowlifes down. We can't have another Scarface situation. The government is still embarrassed about that entire situation. Did we ever get anything on his cousin King? Or Gotti and his crew?"

"Not yet boss, but I'm sure we will soon," Roy replied. After a long sigh, James looked at Roy and said, "We need more informants! The FBI can't get to the big dogs. All they keep getting are small timers with no major input to reach the top players."

Roy nodded his head and agreed. "Don't worry; I'm on it, sir. I'll make all the necessary calls right now," he said, walking out of the office.

James walked over to his desk and sat down. His frustration had reached its boiling point. Before coming to Philadelphia, he had worked in the Prosecutor's office in Baltimore. While there he helped to eliminate most of the top drug dealers in the city, but Philly had turned out to be totally different for him. Everyone was crooked, the cops, agents, judges and lawyers were all on someone's payroll. He was determined to take them all down: The good, the bad and the ugly.

Chapter 5
23rd & Jefferson
North Philly

"Who the fuck set me up?" Gotti shouted. Gotti had his .38 pistol down the throat of a terrified man. A few feet away Marvin had two other men facing a wall, with his .9 mm aimed at their heads. The terrified man's name was Ski; a well-known stick-up boy from North Philly. Ski was a tall, dark-skinned man that was once a pro boxer. After his boxing career had ended, he turned to a life of crime. Ski knew all about Gotti's violent reputation. A year earlier Gotti shot and killed one of Ski's homies over a gambling debt. Ski didn't want to be his next victim. Even he knew when he was in the presence of a real gangster.

"I'm gonna ask you again nigga, who the fuck set me up?" Gotti yelled. "I swear man; I don't know about nothing you are talking about! It wasn't my crew; we was all down in South Philly all night!" Ski muttered with the gun in his mouth. Gotti grabbed Ski by the neck and walked him over to the wall.

"If I find out that you bitch asses had anything to do with robbing me I promise you I'm going to kill your punk asses! Then I'm gonna drive down 5th Street and kill your motherfucking mother!"

Ski's eyes were in complete shock. How did Gotti know that my mother lived on 5th Street he thought to himself? He had never been more scared in his entire life. Everyone knew that Gotti and Marvin were crazed lunatics that only talked with their guns. In a burst of pure rage, Gotti aimed his gun at the two men against the wall and shot them both in the legs. Everyone watched as the two men fell to the floor yelling in severe pain.

"Next time it will be in the head!" Gotti said before he and Marvin walked over to the door. "Nigga you better find out who set us up or I'm coming back to see you!" Gotti said, before walking out the door. Ski stood there watching his men bleeding on the floor. With fear all over his face, he was just happy to be alive.

Chapter 6
18th & Hunting Park

On the top floor of a two-story row house, Troy and an attractive light-skinned female were lying naked in bed. They had just finished a round of intense sex. On a small table nearby there were three stacks of hundred dollar bills. The female's name was Joy, and she was one of the sexy bartenders that worked at Nookie's Afterhours Club. For two months, she and Troy had been having a secret sexual affair.

"Look underneath your pillow," Troy said. Joy reached under the pillow and pulled out a small stack of hundred dollar bills. "That's your cut, five G's," "Thanks, Daddy," Joy said, as she put the money inside her pocketbook.

"We been on a roll but do you think we should slow down a little bit? Shit is getting hot on the streets." "We good babe, just keep doing your job. Getting me the info on all them thirsty ass niggas that come to the club trying to talk your pretty pink panties off, then me and my boys will take care of the rest," Troy replied. "I don't trust them guys, and you shouldn't either." "I don't trust them, but they are good for what we need them for. It's the perfect team. Me, you and them four doing all the dirty work."

Before Joy could respond, her cell phone started to ring. She placed her finger on Troy's lip, signaling him to be quiet. "Hey, Daddy. Yes, I will be there soon love. No I'm fine I don't need anything, I'm good," she said, smiling over at Troy. "Love you, bye," Joy said before she ended the call.

"Damn, he really loves his beautiful, sexy fiancé," Troy said, as he laid Joy back on the bed and began to kiss on her breast. "Yes he does, but I love your dick." "You ain't shit Joy, but that's why I mess with you." "Oh and you talking, Mr. Devil himself. If your father ever found out that his son is fucking his fiancé he would kill us both," Joy said. Troy looked deep into Joy's eye's and said, "He won't ever find out if we keep doing it the way we been doing it. Meeting up a few times a week and not overdoing it. If you get pregnant again, then we will get rid of it like we did the first two. Right now it's all about making money and using my connections to make it for us. But it's your job to keep my father happy; he loves you."

"But I love you," Joy replied. "No, you just love the dick and the money," Troy said as he began to lick her clit and send a wave of chills throughout her trembling body.

In the parking lot outside of the Friday's restaurant on City Avenue, Gotti pulled up and parked his Mercedes next to a silver BMW and a black Audi. Three men were standing outside the cars talking. Gotti and Marvin stepped out of the car and approached the men. They all greeted each other with handshakes and brotherly hugs. The three men were

Philly drug kingpin King and his midget partner Biggie, who stood a measly 4' 11" tall, the other man was their top street sergeant Gee, the leader of the Bottom Boyz. King and his partner Biggie were two of the most powerful drug dealers in the entire tri-state area. In fact, it was Biggie that brought Gotti and Marvin into their lucrative organization. They had all been good friends since doing time in juvie.

"Did you find out anything?" King asked Gotti. "Nothing, but I ain't gonna stop until I do! They got me for three bricks and a new pistol!" Gotti fumed. "They got me for four kilos and $260, 000," Gee added.

"Somebody is definitely setting us up!" Biggie said. "Right, and we need to find out who it is before we take another loss," Marvin said. "Don't worry; we will. The streets talk too much," King replied before he pressed the button on his keychain and popped the trunk of the Silver BMW. Inside were 2 Adidas sports bags. "There are five kilos in each bag, just bring me $10,000 for each one and the rest is y'alls."

Everyone knew that a kilo of pure cocaine was worth between $25 and $35 grand on the streets. King was giving them the wholesale price to ease some of the loss they had taken. He did it because he knew that each of them was loyal to him and the organization. He also knew that none of them would hesitate to kill for him if he needed it. Men like Gotti, Marvin, and Gee were rare. Seventy percent of the hustlers, drug dealers, and other criminals would snitch and turn informant for less time. That is why King and Biggie only surrounded themselves with stand-up men that would never dishonor the code of the streets.

After the men had taken the bags of drugs and placed them in their trunks, King and Biggie watched as they drove away.

"We gotta get to the bottom of this Biggie. We can't keep taking any more major hits like this." "Don't worry, Gotti won't stop until he finds out who did this. You know his wild, young ass is crazy!" Biggie replied as they both started laughing. "That boy don't have no pause button," he added.

"That was some real nigga shit that King just did," Marvin said. "That's why it's nothing I wouldn't do for him. He's a real nigga who understands the streets. Not some high society ass nigga just giving out orders. He comes from a good breed. Scarface is his first cousin. They all are some good dudes and Hood legends."

"Right, maybe one day we will be like them," Marvin said. "I don't want to get that big it puts too many targets on your back. The Feds, snitches, stick up boys and more. Running the entire drug game is not for me. I just want to make a few million and get out alive," Gotti said in a serious tone.

"Do you think it's that simple?" "No, but I'm going to at least try before I end up in a cage or box."

"Wassup with Tori?" Marvin said, changing the subject. "We good. I love that girl. She's my rock." "What's up with her pops, he still don't like you?" "No, but fuck him. He don't like me, and I don't like him. The only reason I ain't put a bullet in his head yet is because of Tori." With that said, Gotti turned up the music in the car, letting the hard lyrics of Young Jeezy flow out of the speakers.

Chapter 7
Big Nookie's

Big Nook and his attractive bartender Jazzmin were behind the bar filling the shelves with bottles of vodka, rum, and wine when Joy walked through the door. Tori was in a back office doing some paperwork. Big Nook came from around the counter and gave his beautiful fiancé a soft kiss and a long hug. "How was your morning so far?"

"It's been great so far," Joy replied. "Is your mother feeling any better?" "Yes babe, Mom is doing a lot better, I stayed with her all night," Joy lied. For the past few weeks, she had been lying about her mother's health so she could get away and have sexual rendezvous with Troy.

Jazzmin looked on as Big Nook and Joy walked towards the back of the club. Jazzmin was usually quiet but very observing of her surroundings. She was a 28-year-old, attractive brown-skinned woman. Unlike Joy, Jazzmin was thick and curvaceous. Her hourglass figure had gotten her lots of attention at the club, but her main focus was making money and taking care of her two children back in South Philly. Jazzmin knew a lot about what was going on at the club, the good and the bad. She knew almost every gangster, pimp, drug dealer and stick-up boy that walked through the doors. They had all tried to get in her panties. Some succeeded, and each one that did paid for it. But Jazzmin had lots of secrets that she wouldn't reveal. A few that had been constantly troubling her. If she could, she would leave Nookie's far behind, but the money was too good to pass up. Being a bartender at a popular club brought in a lot of under the table cash.

Inside a small office in the back of the club, Big Nook was standing against the wall with his pants down to his ankles. Down on her knees, Joy had her hands clutching his ass cheeks giving him one of her amazing blowjobs. When Big Nook had finally come she swallowed every drop of his cum into her warm, wet mouth. "I love my daily protein shake," she smiled.

Chapter 8
26th & Ridge Avenue
North Philly

Kirby's Barbershop was one of the most popular shops in North Philly. Located in the heart of North Philly it was a stable for young and older black males, getting fresh cuts and good conversation on a regular.

Today the crowd inside the shop was boisterous. Everyone was talking about the upcoming Floyd Mayweather fight. When the door opened, and Gotti and Marvin walked inside the crowd got almost dead silent.

"We don't want any trouble!" one of the barbers said. "We are not here for any trouble," Marvin replied. Gotti stood in the middle of the shop and said, "I'm sure most of y'all probably heard by now that I was robbed yesterday. I'm here to give away a $5,000 reward for anyone that has any info on who was responsible."

Gotti placed a small, white card on the shelf and said, "Here's a number to contact me." Then just like that he and Marvin walked out of the barbershop.

"That's one crazy ass nigga right there!" one of the barbers said. "They are both crazy. I heard Marvin murdered his own cousin for some money he owed him." "Somebody is going to die for robbing Gotti. He been on a rampage lately. That nigga ain't got no soul," a customer said. "Whoever robbed him should have killed him. They let the wrong two niggas live!" a teenager said.

Back inside the car Marvin looked over at Gotti and said, "Okay, where to next?" "South Philly, I'm going to go holla at my father," Gotti replied.

"You serious?" Marvin asked as he pulled off. "I'm positive. He is still who he is. Our personal relationship has nothing to do with this situation. I need answers, and maybe he can help us."

"What about going to see Coolie?" Marvin asked. "We will tomorrow afternoon, but today I'm going to see my father. If anything is going down in South Philly, he would know."

Chapter 9
60th & Locust
West Philly

Inside a home on the corner of 60th Street, Troy was seated at a table with four other men. "I got another sucka for y'all. His name is Black. He got a stash house where he keeps his guns, drugs and money out in Southwest Philly. I heard that he's there every night between 10 pm and midnight."

"Good shit Troy and thanks for all the suckas and wanna be gangsters that you put us on," one of the men said. "We will make sure you are taken good care of after we do the hit," another guy said.

After discussing a few more key details, all five men left the house. When they got back inside their vehicles, Troy watched as the four men drove off. When they had disappeared from his sight, Troy walked over to his Lexus and got inside. A young man named Fonz was patiently waiting.

"Man, wassup with them dudes?" Fonz said as Troy pulled away. "Some guys I've been making a lot of money with." "All money ain't good money homeboy." "I got this Fonz. Now do you want the work or not?"

"Yeah, I need it ASAP," Fonz said as he took out a brown bag full of cash from under his black leather jacket. "Look underneath your seat." Fonz reached under his seat and pulled out a small backpack. "That's a whole brick. Shit ain't been touched or stepped on."

Fonz looked at the kilo of cocaine and said, "Damn homie, you really selling me this for just $15 grand?" he asked surprisingly. "Yup, it's all yours Fonz." "Do you got any more?" He asked. "Not yet, but as soon as I come across more you're the first nigga I'm gonna call. Just keep the cash coming, and I'll keep the drugs flowing," Troy said with a devilish smile.

"I'm cool with that." Twenty minutes later, Troy pulled up on the corner of 36th & Spruce Street. He watched as Fonz got out of the car and climbed into a red Cadillac where a beautiful female was patiently waiting for him.

Chapter 10
D.A. Office
Downtown Philadelphia

Candice Shaw was the District Attorney for Philadelphia. For four years she had been a no-nonsense, hard on crime advocate for the D.A. office. She had a spotless record for bringing down some of the most violent murderers, rapists, pedophiles and drug dealers in the city.

Before becoming a D.A. she was a captain on the Philadelphia Police Department, working mostly in the violent crimes and homicide division. Standing at just 5' 2" tall Candice was considered a giant among her peers. She was a short white woman with a cold heart towards all criminals. Inside a large conference room, Candice was surrounded by a group of police lieutenants, Federal agents, and the Police Commissioner.

"This is a list of the top drug dealers and most violent criminals in Philadelphia. Darius "King" Smith, Simon "Black Gotti" Carter, Marvin Washington, Joseph Falcone, Darnell "Gee" Miller, Wallace "Ski" Tucker, Sarah "Sissy" Matthews and Ricardo "Killa" Gomez. By the end of next year, I want a grand jury indictment for everyone on this list. It's time to stop letting these low life criminals control our once beautiful city. I've contacted my friends over at the FBI and DEA offices, and they are willing to help us with any assistance we need to arrest and convict these criminals and get them off our streets! I will keep everyone in the loop on this matter and brief you on any new information as it comes in."

After the meeting, everyone left the room and went their separate ways. But one of the lieutenants walked down the hallway and went into an empty bathroom. He checked the stalls twice to make sure he was alone. When he took out his cell phone, he quickly made an emergency call. "Hello, wassup?" King answered.

"I just left the D.A. meeting that I told you about." "So wassup?" King asked. "They got your name on the list, and she's in the process of putting together a secret task force to take you and other members of your crew down. Your friends Gotti and Marvin are also on the list."

"Are there any indictments or grand jury hearings with informants ready to testify?" "No not yet, but I'm sure there will be soon. Informants come a dime a dozen to make deals with the Prosecutor's office. But as far as I know there are no indictments being issued yet, just a list of major names that the D.A. wants off the streets ASAP!"

"Thanks, I'll be sure to stay far from their reach, and I will make sure Gotti and Marvin know as well. We can meet up later today. I'll talk to you soon," King said before he ended the call. The man placed his cell phone back inside his pocket and casually walked out of the bathroom. For two years he had been on King's payroll, and for all the info he had provided he had been well compensated.

Inside his luxurious Downtown Loft, King looked over at his partner Biggie. "The D.A. got us on her list of high-profile drug dealers and criminals, so we gotta stay even more focused and out of their reach. Gotti and Marvin are also on the list."

"I'll let em know, and don't worry our circle is tight, but I will get it tighter," Biggie replied before he turned back to the X-Box and finished playing his basketball game. Biggie wasn't too worried at all; he and King had their own list of names: Crooked cops, Federal agents, and even a District Judge were on the payroll. Drug money paid for lots of information, and both he and King knew that it was the key to staying ten steps ahead of the law. The lucrative drug game was filled with criminals of all kinds, and most of them were Ivy League educated professionals.

Chapter 11
5th & Passyunk
South Philly

The silver BMW pulled up and parked near a bar on the corner. A few Italian men were standing outside having a conversation. "Wait right here," Gotti told Marvin before he opened the door and got out of the car.

Gotti strolled past the men and walked into the bar. It was crowded inside when he entered. Having been there a few times before Gotti walked straight to the back and knocked on a door that had a "Private" sign on it.

"Come on in," a voice said. Gotti opened the door and stepped inside. Sitting in a chair, smoking a Cuban cigar was his father Joseph Falcone, the boss of the Philadelphia Italian Mob. They were almost a spitting image of each other. The only difference was that Gotti had a darker complexion. They shook hands, and Mr. Falcone asked his son to take a seat.

"What brings you down here?" he asked as he blew a thick cloud of smoke in the air. "I need some info." "About what?" "Four stick up boys that are going around robbing drug dealers."

"So you got robbed?" Mr. Falcone asked in a surprised voice. "Yeah, and it was a setup. That's why I'm here to see if you know anybody that's hitting up drug dealers," Gotti replied.

"Not at the moment, but I can get my people on it and let you know something if I come across any info." "How's your mother?"

Gotti looked at his father with a serious expression. He and his father had a love-hate relationship, and they had been distant for years. "Why don't you call and ask her sometime. You gave her two bastard bi-racial kids." "I told you so many times that your mother was just a friend and nothing more. Why do you bring up this bullshit every time I see you? Your mother knew I was married when we met. I was completely honest with her. She knew that I didn't want any kids."

"You mean any black kids, but you continued to fuck her after she had me and my sister. Now you act like none of us exist." "I gave her money for 18 years for Christ sake!" Mr. Falcone vented.

"That was a payoff to keep her quiet. You didn't want your friends to know that you enjoyed fucking black women and that you had a black mistress, living in West Philly, with two black kids. Your reputation on the streets was more important than your fatherly responsibility."

"Like I said, I told Belinda the truth, but instead of getting the abortion that I paid for she bought a goddamn dress and shoes at Macy's! You will never understand how that made me feel!"

Gotti looked at his father and shook his head in disgust. He was proud of his Italian heritage but not too happy with the man that helped to bring him into the world. He was the son of an Italian mobster and a black stripper. So the blood of the streets ran through his veins. Mr. Falcone looked at his son and couldn't help but admire him. He was more like him than his full blooded Italian children with his wife. When he saw Gotti, he saw a younger version of himself. Many times he wished things could've been different and he and his mixed children were closer. But on the streets of South Philly, he was a legend. A notorious killer with a no-nonsense reputation. He had served over 15 years in Federal prison and had never spoken a single word on his co-defendants or anyone else. He was a stand-up man that lived by the code of Omerta.

"I will call you when or if I find out anything that can help you," he said. Gotti reached out, and they shook hands. Before he walked out of the office, Mr. Falcone said, "You be careful out there."

Gotti smiled and said, "Sure will. You do the same." Then just like that, he was gone.

Chapter 12
Nookie's Club
West Philly

From behind the bar, Tori could see everything that was happening inside the club. Whenever she worked the bar, she paid close attention to her surroundings. Plus having her father's back was a top priority. There were a lot of people that had been jealous of her father's success. He had run a few competitors out of business, and now he had haters praying on his downfall. But as long as he paid off the local police Big Nook's club was untouchable.

    Tori looked around and noticed her brother Troy over by a door talking to the other bartenders Jazzmin and Joy. Lately, it has become a common occurrence. She knew her brother Troy better than anyone, and most times he was up to no good. While serving a customer, Tori saw her ex-boyfriend and his friend walk through the door. His name was Sharif, and he was a known drug boss from Germantown. Standing at six ft 2 inches tall, Sharif could easily pass as a male model for Ebony Magazine. He had a dark complexion with an athletic body, and most women couldn't resist his smooth charm.

    "Wassup boo?" Sharif said approaching Tori at the bar. "I'm not your boo anymore! Tell it to the bitch that you cheated on me for," she said rolling her eyes.

Sharif reached and grabbed Tori's hand. She snatched it away and said, "Stop playing yourself before I tell my boyfriend."

Sharif smirked and said, "Fuck your boyfriend. My gun bust too!" Sharif was showing off for the onlookers around the bar. He knew all about Gotti's notorious reputation. They had beef in the past after Gotti had been acquitted of murdering Sharif's cousin.

Before Tori could respond Big Nook walked over and said, "Sharif, go enjoy yourself young man. Don't want no trouble tonight." Sharif looked at Tori and winked his eye before he turned and walked over to the poker table where his friend was waiting. Tori shook her head in disgust. She couldn't stand Sharif's ass anymore. He had been mentally and physically abusive in their relationship. He had also cheated on her with numerous women many times and had given her gonorrhea before she finally called it off and left him for good. She knew that if she ever told Gotti about his disrespect that Sharif would be a dead man.

Tori wasn't well liked at the club. She couldn't stand Joy, because she felt like she was a young gold digger, taking advantage of her older father. Though she knew Joy wasn't right, she had never found out any real info to prove it. She just trusted her intuition.

As for Jazzmin, they were cordial, but Tori didn't trust her either. She was too quiet, and there was something very sneaky about her that didn't sit well with Tori. The only person she liked at the club was the janitor Country. He was a heavyset, dark-skinned 28-year old that moved to Philly from Durham, North Carolina. He did his job every night and minded his business.

Chapter 13
58th & Greenway Avenue
Southwest Philly

The four masked men had been watching the small house for the past two hours. They had placed a GPS locator on the man's car and secretly followed him home, just like they had done with all the other drug dealers they had robbed. The hits were sweet. Troy got them the jobs and names of the dealers, and they did all the rest. The breakdown was always the same, 70-30 split of everything they had taken from the drug dealers. They were the best at their jobs. Knowing that drug dealers wouldn't go to the police after being robbed made it even sweeter.

After surrounding the home, the four men kicked down the front and back doors and charged in with guns blazing. They caught everyone inside completely off guard. After tying everyone up and taking Black upstairs they emptied his safe, then pistol whipped Black until he fell unconscious. In less than fifteen minutes they were out the door, speeding off in their stolen mini-van. With 5 kilos and $97,000 in cash inside a duffel bag, they made another clean getaway.

Meanwhile, in North Philly

Computer geek Roscoe had looked over the surveillance video numerous times. He had written down many notes about the four masked men that robbed Gotti and Marvin. Twenty minutes later, Gotti and Marvin showed up at his home, and Roscoe told them everything he noticed about the masked culprits.

"I researched the video thoroughly, and from my personal conclusion I believe two of the robbers were black and the other two were either Latino or white. Neither of them had on any gloves and after I magnified the footage, I noticed instantly that the men were of different races. Also, the two black robbers were wearing the new Air Jordan's and the other two men were wearing black Adidas. Also, one of the black robbers is left-handed, that's the hand he held his gun in." Roscoe said.

"Damn, that's some good shit, Roscoe!" Marvin said. "That's not all. Come up closer to the monitor and check this out," he said. Both Gotti and Marvin moved their chairs up closer to the computer screen.

Roscoe then grabbed the computer mouse and pressed a button that magnified one of the masked gunmen's eyes. "One of the black robbers has green eyes. I enhanced the footage to 100% to make sure I was accurate. So fellas there you have it. Your robbers are four men. Two black and two either Spanish or white. Two wore Jordan's, and two wore Adidas. One left handed and has piercing green eyes." Roscoe said before he stood up from his chair.

Gotti was excited, but he didn't show it. His serious facial expression stayed the same. After paying

Roscoe for the good work, he had done Gotti and Marvin walked out the front door and got back in the car. "We have to find these niggas and show them that they robbed the wrong niggas!" Gotti said, as he started up the car and drove down the street. "And more importantly we need to find out the mastermind behind it all," he added. "We will! We definitely will," Marvin said. With that said they headed back towards Northeast Philly.

Chapter 14
Nookie's Club

Country walked through the boisterous crowd of hustlers, gamblers and fast women. He went inside the men's bathroom and took out his cell phone, and started to text someone.

Yo homie so far it's been quiet, just full of the regulars. But tonight the guy Sharif came in and had a few words with Tori. Didn't get to hear what was said but Tori didn't look happy. Also, something is going on around here, seems like everyone is full of secrets. I will keep you posted.

Moments later, a text came back to Country's cell phone.

Thanks, homie.

Country put his phone back in his pocket and walked out of the bathroom. For months he had been secretly working for someone who had major interest on what went on at the club. For his information, he was paid very well.

Troy walked around the club watching very closely. He kept an eye on all the big gamblers and drug bosses. He stood back from the tables as they dropped thousands of dollars as if it was nothing. Bosses as far as New York, Miami and Chicago were dropping loads of money on the poker and craps tables.

Troy took mental notes on every one of them. While they were inside enjoying themselves, he had already had small GPS locators attached to the bottom of their parked luxury cars.

    Big Nook had a private parking lot adjacent to the club's building for all of the high rollers. Troy was the person in charge of the parking lot. From there he would begin his plots and schemes. Once he gathered all the info on the individuals, he would put his four-man robbery team on them. Only a few people had known about Troy's secret plots. His father Big Nook was not one of them. In so many instances Big Nook had been his savior. Over the years many people had tried to hurt or kill Troy. He was a known devious crook and was very unlikable by many. But because he was Big Nook's son he had gotten lots of passes.

Chapter 15
Later That Night

Sharif and his friend Mike left the club and got inside their separate cars. After Mike pulled off, Sharif pulled out of the parking lot and drove away in the opposite direction. A few blocks away he pulled up to the corner of 49th & Hoops Street and parked his Lexus behind a tinted, black van. After exiting his car, Sharif walked over to the van and pulled open the sliding door. When he stepped inside, there were two FBI agents waiting for him.

"Find anything good tonight?" one of the agents asked. "I came across a few ballers and some out of town high rollers. They were spending lots of money," Sharif said.

"What's up with Big Nook and his son?" "Big Nook looks clean, but his son is up to something." "Did anyone from King's drug organization come through there?" one of the agents asked, as he started removing the wired belt buckle from around Sharif's waist. The Gucci belt buckle had a small listening device attached to it, recording everything in its surrounding area.

"I didn't see anyone from King's organization in there tonight. I'm surprised that Gee, Black, Ski, or Gotti wasn't in there tonight. Maybe next time," Sharif replied.

"That's fine, we will meet up tomorrow around six o'clock, and have you wired up again," the agent told him.

Sharif nodded his head and stepped out of the FBI undercover surveillance van. When he got back into his car he felt disgusted with himself. Three months earlier he had been arrested in Germantown with two guns and a kilogram of crack cocaine. With his prior drug convictions, he was facing a life sentence in a federal penitentiary. Instead of taking his case to trial, he decided to cooperate with the Feds and work for them on the streets. They had promised him a get out of jail free card if he could help them bring in some major players. Gotti and Marvin were just a few of the men on his list. He had a personal hatred and vendetta against Gotti for killing his cousin a few years back.

Chapter 16
The Next Day

Donna Carter was drop dead gorgeous. Standing at 5 foot 7 inches, she had the perfect hourglass figure. Her long, silky black hair fell down to the center of her back, and her beautiful light skinned face brought out her exotic Italian and black features. Donna was Gotti's younger sister by 3 years. She was 24, with no children and had a well-paying job as a real estate agent for Century 21. She had been the only person whom Gotti used to purchase his homes. She was just one of a handful of the people Gotti trusted with his life.

Driving her new red Cadillac SRX Donna pulled up to the corner of 56th & Market and double parked. A few moments later, her boyfriend Fonz walked out of a bar and got inside the vehicle. "Wassup babe?" Fonz said, before kissing her lips.

"Working babe! Getting rid of all this work." Fonz smiled, then reached inside his pocket and pulled out a stack of hundred dollar bills. "Troy has been hooking me up with some unbelievable prices."

"You really need to stop messing with him. You know my brother can't stand his bitch ass!" Donna said as she pulled off down Market Street.

"It's cool babe, plus he got the lowest prices in the city. I'm making triple my money since I started copping from Troy."

"When did his snake ass become a connect? He never sold weight before," Donna asked. "I don't know and I don't care as long as he keeps selling me kilos for 15 grand."

Donna stopped her Cadillac at a red light and said, "Just watch yourself and definitely watch that snake nigga Troy. He is no good, and everyone knows it. Don't let him get you caught up in this mess. And please don't ever mention or say my brother's name around him. I don't trust him!"

"I never did and I won't babe. I promise." Fonz assured her. "Now can we please stop talking about Troy and go downtown to Del Frisco's to eat?"

"You ain't saying nothing but a word," Donna said as she made a quick U-turn and headed towards Chestnut Street. "I'm starving," she smiled.

Chapter 17
State Road
Northeast Philly

The Curran-Fromhold Correctional Facility is located on State Road, with a few other violent Philadelphia prisons. In the past year, the Philly prison system had been corrupted by crooked correctional officers and high officials. There had been a long list of indicted employees for smuggling drugs and cell phones into the prisons. Gotti was patted down and escorted into the visitation room where his tall younger cousin Coolie was patiently waiting for him.

    Gotti took a seat beside Coolie and gave him a hug. "You been good?" "Hell no! It's fucked up in here! Niggas beefing with each other all day long! North Philly niggas beefing with South Philly niggas! West Philly niggas beefing with everybody else! Shit is fucked up man!" Coolie stood 6'3 and had a dark brown complexion, with a small teardrop tattoo below his left eye.

    "I'm on it Coolie just give me a little more time cuz, just chill," Gotti said. "Chill! Are you serious G?" Coolie leaned over and placed his mouth to Gotti's ear. "I took this case for you! You shot that cop, not me! Luckily he didn't die, but if that cop wakes up from that coma and points me out I'm getting the death penalty. They won't give me bail because they are waiting to see what happened with the cop. The fucking D.A. has already offered me two deals if I plead guilty to the attempted murder."

"Look, Coolie; I said that I'm on it. I got you one of the best lawyers in the city, and he told me that without the officer's testimony that they have no other evidence against you and you will be set free." Gotti said.

"So I guess I'm going to be here until the cop wakes up from his coma and points me out to a racist ass all white jury!"

"Don't worry about it Coolie; I said I'm on it. Just give me some time and I will get you out of here. I know what you did for me, but you know I would have done the same for you." Gotti said in a serious tone.

Coolie knew that Gotti's words were real and sincere. Gotti had basically raised his younger cousin. After Coolie's parents were both gunned-down in a West Philly bar one night Gotti had taken in his younger cousin and put him under his wing. They were like brothers, and it was killing Gotti to see Coolie in his current situation for something he didn't do. Gotti had shot the police officer once in the head, but it was Coolie that got caught with a gun a few blocks away. Even though the gun Coolie had wasn't the weapon that was used in the actual shooting, he was black, and he matched the physical description that officers were searching for.

With Coolie's previous arrest record, drug and gang affiliation with the King organization, it was enough for the D.A.'s office to charge him with the attempted murder of a Philadelphia police officer. They had a weak case against Coolie, and the D.A. needed the officer to wake from his coma to identify him as the shooter for a conviction to stick. So at present Ryan "Coolie" Carter was being held without bail.

"So what's this I'm hearing…you got robbed? It's all over the jail that someone set you and Marv up for a major hit." Gotti looked at Coolie with a surprised expression. "You heard about it in here?" "I told you that it's all over the pods. Niggas talk like bitches in here. Plus these crooked ass C-O's can't keep they mouths shut either. Are you good out there?"

"I'm fine. And I'm going to find out who did it, trust me!" Gotti said. "I need you to keep your ears open for any info that can lead me to the niggas who set me up."

"Don't worry Gotti, I already been on it for you. You just do what you need to do and get me the fuck out of this hell hole. CFCF is the worst, and I can't eat another Chee-Chee," Coolie said, as they both started laughing.

Twenty minutes later, Gotti gave Coolie a hug, and he was escorted out by a C-O that he knew "keep an eye on him," he said. "Don't worry Gotti; I got Coolie up in here. He as good as gold," the C-O assured him.

When Gotti got back into the car, Marvin noticed the serious expression on his face.

"Is Coolie good?" Gotti nodded his head and said, "Yeah, for now, but we gotta get him out ASAP! So you know what we have to do now." "Go see Stan?" Marvin asked. "Right," Gotti replied.

Chapter 18
18th & Snyder
South Philly

Troy sat back with a big smile on his face. On a large round table in front of him was four kilos of pure cocaine and $85,000 in cash. Troy and his four robber friends were dividing the profits from the late night robbery of Black in Southwest Philly.

"This was it?" Troy asked as he placed his share inside of a Nike duffle bag. "That's all we found," one of the men lied. The truth was they had kept a kilo and another $12 grand in cash for themselves.

"Cool," Troy said. "I heard that Black is still in the hospital with some severe head trauma." "Fuck him! Now who is next?" one of the men asked. "I know this guy named Fonz from West Philly. He is getting a couple of dollars on 46th, 48th, and 49th Streets. I got a location on him," Troy said.

"Ain't that your friend you been selling the drugs to?" one of the men asked. "Ain't no friends in this game!" Troy replied as he looked each man straight in their eyes. "It's a dog-eat-dog world, and I'm one of the red-nosed pits."

With that said each of the men left the house and went their separate ways. Troy had called and set up a two-kilo sale with Fonz. The same drugs he had planned to steal back from him.

Big Nook and Joy had just returned from the Cherry Hill Mall in New Jersey. After a profitable weekend at the club he decided to treat her to a shopping spree at the mall. Joy had made sure she purchased the best fashions her sugar daddy's money could buy. Gucci, Versace, Prada and Vera Wang just to name a few. Big Nook didn't have a problem spoiling his attractive, much younger fiancé. She was everything he wanted in a woman, and the sex with her was mind-blowing. In his eyes, Joy could do no wrong.

The sad part about their situation was that Joy had been in a secret sexual relationship with Big Nook's own son Troy, and had even been impregnated by him. She was a woman of greed, lust and betrayal, and all her life she had been using her beauty to seduce and control men.

Chapter 19
Temple Hospital
North Philly

Gotti and Marvin were sitting inside the BMW, right across the street from the hospital. They had been out there patiently waiting for a half hour. Suddenly a short, skinny brown skinned man walked out of the front entrance carrying a black backpack. He approached the car, opened the back door and got inside.

After passing the backpack to Marvin, he said, "Here's everything you will need. Are y'all sure this is what y'all want to do?" Stan asked.

Gotti looked at Stan with serious eyes and said, "This is what we are going to do!" "Well, I gave y'all all the info you will need, and I'm going to do my part to help," Stan said before he shook their hands and got out of the car. After Stan had walked back into the hospital, Gotti drove away.

"When do you want to do this?" "Stan said tomorrow is the best day to do it because there will be less staff working," Gotti replied.

Marvin shook his head and said, "I'm ready homie, now just drop me off over my shorty's spot, and I'll see you tomorrow morning."

"No problem," Gotti said as he drove down Broad Street, headed towards South Philly.

54th & Baltimore Avenue, Southwest Philly

Sharif pulled up and parked his car behind a black Ford Taurus. He quickly got out then got into the front seat of the Taurus. "Wassup Gee?" "Wassup Sharif, you got that?" Sharif zipped down his jacket and took out a large stack of hundred dollar bills.

"That's 50 stacks for two birds," Sharif said. "There's a Popi store off 58th Street, just go there and ask for two chicken platters, they are there waiting for you."

Gee was speaking in code to throw off anyone that could've been listening. Even though he had been serving Sharif for a while, he still didn't trust a soul in the drug game. King had taught him always to be suspicious. That your closest friend would quickly turn on you if he or she wasn't built to stand the pressure from authorities.

"Okay, I'm on my way up there now," Sharif said before he stepped out of the car and rushed back towards his own car. He watched as Gee sped off down the street. Ten minutes later, Sharif was inside the Popi store picking up two kilos of cocaine. They were packaged neatly inside of the two white Styrofoam food containers. Less than a half hour later, he was turning in the two kilos of cocaine, and his wired Gucci belt device into the hands of the FBI.

Without knowing, Gee had been set up by Sharif, who was working for the Feds. It was Sharif's third time copping weight from Gee. The Feds were using

Sharif to help build a major case against Gee and the King drug organization. The plan was to get as much evidence against Gee so that he had no choice but to snitch on his boss King. Sharif was the government's pawn to take down King. Once his job was done he was promised a sweet deal in the Federal Witness Protection Program, also known as the Witness Security Program or WITSEC. Sharif would rather break the code of the streets and become a government informant, then spend a life sentence behind bars.

"Good job Sharif," one of the agents said. "This gets us one step closer to the big fishes like King, Biggie, Gotti, and Marvin."

"The prosecutor is really going to love this," another agent added. When Sharif got back in his car he drove off and pulled over a few blocks away. He felt bad for being a snitch. It was eating at him daily. The only person who had known about his current situation was his best friend, Mike. Sharif had told him everything that had happened. Mike understood because six years earlier he had been a top street informant, working for the DEA. Mike had informed on so many people that he got his 30-year prison sentence reduced to a 4 and a half year sentence, at a Federal prison camp in Lewisburg, Pennsylvania. After a long sigh, Sharif pulled off down the street, heading towards Mike's house.

Chapter 20
24th & Tasker
South Philly

Marvin was somewhere lost between Earth and heaven. With his eyes closed tight, he relaxed back into the sofa enjoying the amazing blowjob that Jazzmin was giving him. They had been in a sexual relationship for the past four months. Jazzmin wanted more than sex. She was deeply attracted to Marvin. His attitude, demeanor, and swag drove her crazy. She had never been with a man who had touched every single part of her mind, body, and soul.

As for Marvin, he was physically attracted to Jazzmin, but beyond sex, he wasn't interested in anything else. Marvin could feel the intense orgasm quickly coming. When he opened his eyes, he watched as Jazzmin gripped her hand around his dick and began to swallow every single drop of his warm, thick cum into her waiting mouth. She could feel his entire body trembling all over.

Jazzmin then grabbed Marvin's hand and together they tiptoed passed the bedroom of her sleeping children and into her bedroom. She undressed Marvin and then slipped off her silk, black nightie and joined him in her large, king sized bed. For the next hour and a half, they fucked like two wild animals. The sex was amazing for them both. On that level, there were no complaints. When they had finally drained all the energy from each other's bodies, Jazzmin laid her head on Marvin's muscular chest.

"What's going on down at the club?" he asked. "Same old shit. Big Nook chasing Joy around, Troy chasing money and Tori chasing niggas away," she said as they both started laughing.

"And who are you chasing?" Jazzmin started kissing Marvin on his chest and then she said, "The only person I'm chasing is you." After twenty minutes of pillow talk, they were both knocked out in each other's arms.

North Philly

"Oh god! Yes! Yes, Daddy take your pussy!!" Joy shouted out. Troy had her bent over the bed, fucking her hard from behind. The truth was that he got pleasure out of fucking his father's fiancé.

"Take this dick bitch! Take all this dick!" He told her. With each stroke, Troy smacked Joy hard on the ass cheeks. Joy had enjoyed the pain. The harder, the better. She was a true undercover freak, with no sexual boundaries. She enjoyed both anal and oral sex, and there was nothing she wouldn't do to please her man, or whoever it was that she was fucking.

After he came Troy put his pants back on and said, "You got to hurry up and get back to the club before my pops starts worrying." "It's cool babe, I told him that I was leaving for a while to go check up on my mom," Joy replied.

"Well, I have to get back to the club. Some more high rollers are coming through tonight." Troy said, before he placed a stack of money on the nightstand and rushed out the door. Joy looked at the stack of money she had earned from doing her part in the robberies and smiled. Then she laid back on the bed and began to masturbate.

8th and Mifflin Street, South Philly

In the basement of a small row home, Mr. Falcone watched as the tied-up, beaten and bruised man laid on the floor in a pool of his own blood. Mr. Falcone stood over the man, holding an aluminum baseball bat. "You fucking rat! You didn't think that I would find out you were working with the Feds!!" Mr. Falcone raised the bat high in the air and started smashing the man's head in. "You fucking rat!!" he yelled out.

Standing a few feet away was his underboss Vic. Even he couldn't stomach the severe beating that the man was receiving. Blood and bone matter were splattered all over the floor and walls. It was total brutality and slaughter.

"Die you rat!" After Mr. Falcone was done, he had his men take the man's corpse across the Ben

Franklin Bridge to New Jersey. They were instructed to bury him in a Camden City trash dump.

Chapter 21
12th & Somerset
North Philly

Stan Lewis was a man full of many secrets. As a hard working RN at Temple, he was well liked by the staff. But his other side was completely different. Much darker. For over a year Stan had been addicted to heroin. The drug had him strung out, but he managed to hide his addiction at work and from most of his family and friends. Gotti and Marvin knew all about Stan's weakness to heroin. They also knew how important it was to use Stan's heroin addiction to their advantage. They promised him $2500 and a quarter ounce of pure uncut heroin. It was a deal that Stan couldn't refuse. He was a junkie; and junkies had no control over the drugs that consumed their bodies.

Sitting on the bathroom floor, Stan had a small belt wrapped tightly around his left arm and a syringe in his right hand. He was sweating profusely and his eyes were bloodshot. When he found his vein, he stuck the syringe full of heroin into it, letting the drug flow through his body. Moments later, Stan was laid out on the bathroom floor, in a serene place where he wished he could stay at forever.

~~~

King picked up his ringing cell phone and said, "Wassup? Any good news?" "Yes, I have some news that can potentially help you and your entire crew," the male voice said. King listened as his secret source told him everything he had recently found out. When he was done King said, "Thanks for everything. Your payment will be ready for you tomorrow." Then both lines went dead.

King looking over at his partner Biggie said, "My plug in the FBI just got me a list of names, places, and things we need to be aware of."

"That's good! We need to kill every rat in the city!!" Biggie replied with anger in his voice. "These rats are fucking up the game! There are no more stand-up men! The rats put them all away in prison!"

King shook his head and said, "Calm down Lil' homie. The rats will get what's coming to them."

The Next Day

Candice Shaw was obsessed with bringing all criminals to justice. She was determined to lock up every single crook in the city of Philadelphia. Only a few people had known the true reason for her hatred towards criminals. Twenty years earlier, when she was an 18-year-old freshman at Drexel University, she had come home early one day to receive the shock of her life. Her parent's northeast home had been robbed and ransacked.

When she ran upstairs and entered the master bedroom, Candice couldn't believe her teary eyes. Both of her parents were lying next to each other, each shot in the head. Her father's throat had been cut, and his tongue had been removed from his mouth. The tragic sight had devastated Candice. For years she needed psychological help to cope with the nightmares and mental damage she constantly suffered with. Since that horrible day, Candice had never been the same again. Her life would take a major turn, and now the once proud Engineering major had changed her major to Criminal Justice.

Four years later, she had graduated at the top of her class. Two months after graduating Candice was working as an assistant in the D.A.'s downtown office. She was determined to make a change, and deep down inside she wanted to find the culprits behind her parent's brutal murder.

But whoever was responsible was a pro. They left no clues, evidence or any DNA behind. For twenty years she had been haunted by the double homicide of her elderly parents. Now she took her personal pain out on every criminal that crossed her path. Justice is what she lived for. She didn't care about the overcrowding prison population that was destroying America's prison system. She didn't care about two and three inmates living in one cell together. If she could, she would put fifty inmates in a cell and throw away the key. She hated criminals with a passion, seeing them rot behind bars was the light inside her dark soul.

Chapter 22
60th & Chester Avenue
Southwest Philly

Black was back on the streets with a vengeance. After he was robbed by the four masked men and beaten unconscious, he was determined to find out who the people responsible were.

Black had a few people on his list that he believed were involved. Only a few individuals had known of his whereabouts, and there were only two people he had copped drugs from in the past month. That was Gotti and his friend Marvin. Black wanted revenge. He felt disrespected to the highest degree. The major loss had put him back at square one. Everything he had saved for was now gone.

Black sat down on the couch, gripping his brand new Heckler and Koch HK416 assault rifle. Murder was not new to him at all. He had served a seven-year sentence for a manslaughter conviction when he was a juvenile.

After placing the rifle inside of a black duffel bag, Black left the apartment and got inside his tinted black Chevy Impala. Somebody had to die for the pain they caused him. Black wanted answers, and he wouldn't rest until the men behind his robbery had met their maker.

Chester, PA

For the past few days, Ski had been laying low in the small city of Chester. After the incident with Gotti and Marvin, he decided to relocate and get his mind right. He feared Gotti but knew he had to do something about the way he had been disrespected by him.

Gotti had shot his two friends in the legs for no reason at all. When the word hit the streets Ski, and his crew had become the laughing stock of the neighborhood. Ski was totally embarrassed. At the end of the day, he was still a man. Once, one of the most feared men in boxing.

Ski knew that he couldn't rest until Gotti and Marvin were both dead. He was tired of hiding out acting like a scared dog with his tail between his legs. He felt less than a man for being so cowardly. But today fearing Gotti and Marvin would change. After kissing his girlfriend Tamia on the lips, Ski loaded his Glock and headed back to North Philly to pick up his crazy cousin, Gucci.

Chapter 23
Later That Evening

Inside a black Lexus, Gotti and Marvin were parked across the street from Temple Hospital. They both exited the car wearing doctor scrubs, with stethoscopes around their necks. Roscoe had made them each a fake hospital ID for access into the facility without any hassle. They walked through the front entrance and passed Stan who was sitting at the front desk. He nodded as they walked by. Together they got into the elevator, and Marvin pressed the button to the third floor. Stan had given them all the info they needed to finish their task. They were both focused and determined to complete their mission. It was life or death.

Inside their pockets were loaded 9mm's with attached silencers. When they stepped off the elevator the loudspeaker came on, and a man's voice said, "Will Officer Daniels, please come to the front desk."

As Gotti and Marvin walked down the hall towards their destination, they watched as a black police officer walked right past them. When they had approached room 340, they quickly stepped inside. After Marvin had closed the curtain, Gotti took out his weapon and aimed it at the patient's head. The comatose patient was Officer Calvin Jones, the same man that Gotti had shot a few months earlier.

He had been in a coma ever since the shooting occurred. Doctors were not sure if he would make it or not. The bullets had severely damaged most of his internal organs. Officer Jones was the key piece and link to put Coolie away for a life sentence or on death row. Gotti couldn't let that happen. Coolie was like his little brother, and seeing him rot in a cold prison cell for the rest of his life wasn't a part of the plan.

While Marvin stayed by the door, looking out for anyone entering the room, Gotti had his 9mm pointing at the man's temple. Gotti looked around the room and noticed all the working monitors and machines that were keeping Officer Jones alive. Gotti put the gun back into his pocket and then he started snatching tubes and unplugging all the machines.

After he snatched the breathing device from Officer Jones's nose and mouth his body began to tremble uncontrollably. All the air, water and blood that he needed to stay alive had completely stopped flowing through his system. In less than ten minutes Officer Jones was dead.

Gotti felt his pulse to make sure he was gone. When he was positive, he replaced all the tubes and re-plugged the machines. He wanted everything to look the same. With latex glove on he wasn't concerned about leaving any DNA evidence behind for forensics to discover.

His first plan was to shoot him, but Gotti realized that unplugging the machines would be a lot easier to complete the job without any traces of foul play. The plan to get rid of Officer Jones was a lot easier than he had originally thought.

In less than ten minutes Gotti and Marvin were walking back down the hall. As they headed back to the elevator doctors and nurses were rushing towards the room. When they stepped into the elevator, Officer Daniels was stepping off and rushing down the hall as well. It was his security duty to keep an eye on his fellow officer and good friend.

When Gotti and Marvin walked back past the front desk, Stan smiled and nodded his head. He had done his job and would be compensated greatly for his role. Calling the officer on the loud speaker was the key to their successful mission. Gotti and Marvin exited the building and walked back to their car. The job was now complete, and both men could finally breathe a sigh of relief.

Marvin started up the car, and they pulled off onto Broad Street. No words were spoken as they headed towards their next destination. They both knew that it was still a long road ahead of them. There were still four men out there who robbed them; and the celebration could wait until they were found and dealt with.

Chapter 24
Chew & Chelten Avenue
Germantown

Across the street from the Crown Fried Chicken restaurant, Sharif was inside a small row home with two known drug dealers. Their names were Ricardo "Killa" Gomez and his partner Sarah "Sissy" Matthews. They were two of the biggest meth and ecstasy dealers in the tri-state area.

Sharif had just purchased a hundred thousand dollars' worth of ecstasy and two AR-15 assault rifles. Unbeknownst to Killa and Sissy, Sharif was wired and recording the entire conversation. It was his second major drug purchase in the past two weeks. Sharif didn't have any picks of who he had to set up. As long as it got him a sweet deal with the Federal Prosecutor, everybody was a target. He made it very clear that he wasn't serving a life sentence for anyone.

Twenty minutes later, Sharif was walking out of the house carrying two large briefcases, filled with drugs and guns. When Sharif made it back to the FBI surveillance van, the two agents were overly excited.

"You are on a roll Sharif," one of the agents said. "This will definitely get you your 5K1 motion. This is more than substantial assistance; the Prosecutor will see to it that you should benefit for all of your cooperation," another agent replied.

Sharif nodded his head and smiled. The thought of serving one day in prison was scary. He had lots of enemies in the Federal and state prison systems that wouldn't hesitate to put a shank through his heart. For a while there had been some whispers on the streets that Sharif was a rat, working with the Feds. But no one had any proof that Sharif was an informant. The government had kept their star street informant a secret. He had turned out to be a valuable asset.

After dropping off the drugs, Sharif got out of the van and got back into his car. Twenty minutes later, Sharif was meeting up with his friend Mike at the Bonefish Grill restaurant.

Lehigh Avenue, North Philly

Gucci spotted his cousin Ski as soon as he pulled up in front of the door. With a large green duffel bag in his arms, he quickly got inside the car and shut the door. "Wassup cuz?" Gucci said. "It's been a long while since you needed my help," he smiled. Seeing the serious look on Ski's face, he asked, "So what's wrong?"

"I need your help cuz. Some niggas named Gotti and Marvin ran up on me and my boys. They shot two of them for no reason."

"Enough said, let's give them both a dirt nap," Gucci said, taking out his AK-47 assault rifle. "It's not that simple. Gotti and Marvin are both gangsters and major drug dealers in the King organization."

"They work for King?" Gucci asked curiously. "Yes, King and his partner Biggie, do you know them?" Gucci sat back and shook his head. "Yeah, I know them both very well."

"From where?" Ski asked. "I used to be a part of their crew a few years ago. Right before I caught my Lil' drug case and served that 18-month bid on State Road."

"Well Gotti works for them, but I don't give a fuck. They need to die for what they did to me and my crew," Ski said. "Well we might need my B.O.D. crew," Gucci said.

"Naw man. They are too reckless. Me and you can handle this by ourselves." "Fuck it; I'm down cuz. We blood, so it's whatever," Gucci replied.

"Cool, I'm heated right now. So let's go do a few stickups to calm my nerves.

As far as Gotti and Marvin are concerned, we have to lay low until the right moment comes. They are hard to track down, but everyone slips and when they do they are both dead men!" Ski said as he pulled off down the street. Gucci sat back in deep thought. He knew a lot about King and Biggie; they had a long history. With his AK-47 across his lap, Gucci knew that once he killed Gotti and Marvin that a war with King and Biggie was inevitable.

Chapter 25
Northern Liberties

Donna and Fonz were inside the bathroom, taking a warm shower together. They had made love twice under the soothing, warm water. With the radio playing and the water running they never heard the sound of the front door being pushed open. Without them knowing it, the four masked men entered the apartment aiming their loaded guns. While three of the men ran around the apartment looking for drugs and money, one of the men walked towards the bathroom. When he pushed the door open, both Donna and Fonz were completely caught off guard and startled.

"Put your hands up and don't fucking move!" he yelled. "Where's the money Fonz?" "I don't have no money man!"

The masked man aimed his gun at Fonz's leg and shot him. Pow!!! Fonz slumped down in the tub. Donna screamed and tried to help him. They were naked and scared for their lives. "Where's the money Fonz?" he asked again. "I don't have any money!" Fonz told him.

The masked gunman aimed his weapon at Fonz's head. "It's behind the wall clock in the living room!" Donna shouted. The man told one of his men to go check out the wall clock in the living room while he kept an eye on Donna and Fonz. Donna stared deep into his penetrating green eyes. She would remember them as long as she lived.

"Bingo!" a man's voice yelled from another room. Donna leaned down and comforted her bleeding boyfriend. She was more angry than afraid. Suddenly a short man walked into the bathroom carrying a green duffel bag filled with drugs, guns, and cash.

"Let's get out of here Ron!" "Nigga are you crazy?" the man shouted. The short man had just made a critical mistake by saying his friend's name. Donna took note of it but had played it off by crying and holding Fonz, acting as if she didn't hear a thing. Moments later, the four men were running out the door, disappearing into the night. Donna called an ambulance for Fonz's injuries, and then her second call was to her brother Gotti. She had a name for him.

Chapter 26
12th Street
North Philly

Gotti was incensed after hearing the shocking news of his sister and her boyfriend getting robbed, and hearing that they had been robbed by the same four masked men had him even more upset. At least they were still alive he thought to himself, and he had a name to one of the culprits.

Gotti and Marvin parked and got out of the car. They walked over to Stan's house and knocked on the door. He quickly opened the front door and let them both inside. Gotti could plainly see that Stan was high on something. Marvin walked around the messy house surveying everything. When he entered back into the living room, Gotti was standing there talking to Stan. He gave Gotti a nod, letting him know that it was all clear.

Without hesitation, Marvin ran behind Stan and put him in a choke hold. They both fell to the floor, but Marvin continued to hold on tightly while Stan was struggling to free himself. Gotti reached into his pocket and pulled out a large syringe. It was filled with a dose of toxic heroin, enough to overdose and kill whoever injected it into their system. Gotti sat down on Stan's legs and grabbed his arm. Stan was too fatigued to push him off. When Gotti had found a vein, he stuck the syringe into his arm and helped to hold him down.

Seconds later, the poisonous drug was overtaking Stan's entire body. Five minutes later his body stopped moving, and Stan was dead. They then stood up and left his cold body slumped on the floor. Stan had been a dead man the moment he assisted Gotti and Marvin with murdering the cop. They couldn't let a junkie live with their secret. Stan couldn't be trusted, so he had to die. The secrets that he knew could get them both the death penalty if he ever spoke a word to the wrong person. They had killed men for less. For them it wasn't personal at all, it was just business. If you couldn't trust the people you were in business with then, you had to eliminate them. Because Gotti and Marvin both knew that too many people were dead or in prison for trusting the wrong people.

Chapter 27
Two Days Later
The Holiday Inn on City Live Avenue

Inside a small hotel room, Troy laid in bed between two attractive white women. For the past five hours, they had fucked, sucked and used every drug known to man. Cocaine, ecstasy, weed, perks and even crack. Troy had already blown most of the money he had on women, drugs and a new Mercedes Benz he bought with straight cash. He didn't care, there was always a new drug dealer to find, set up and rob. They were a dime a dozen, plus Troy didn't have any future plans; he lived for the moment. Money, women, and drugs ruled his life, and he didn't care what he needed to do to get them.

Troy then reached over and grabbed a glass pipe from a small, wooden table. He then placed a small rock of crack cocaine into the pipe and started burning it with a lighter, before inhaling the crack cocaine into his system. Five minutes later, Troy was high off his ass, enjoying the pleasure of a wonderful dick suck from one of his two tricks.

West Philly

Big Nook removed a large, abstract picture off the wall inside his office. A built in steel wall safe was now on display. He used a small key to open the safe. When the safe opened, there were stacks of cash, jewelry and all the deeds to his properties stuffed inside. He placed four large stacks of hundred dollar bills into the safe.

For years he had been saving up for retirement from the night club business. Big Nook had plans to one day retire and move him and his beautiful young fiancée down to Miami. It had over a million dollars in cash and Tori had a key to get inside of it.

Big Nook grabbed two more stacks of cash off of a table and stuffed them inside the safe with all the rest. His plan was to stack all he could for another six months, then leave Philly far behind.

Chapter 28
Early the Next Morning
North Philly

A swarm of FBI and DEA agents surrounded the small two-story home on 4th & Girard Avenue. This was a normal routine for the Feds, which was to strike the suspects early as they slept peacefully in bed. With an arrest warrant in hand, the Feds had the power to execute and then prosecute any individual on the FBI or DEA fugitive list.

Without any warning, a group of agents kicked in the front door and burst through with weapons drawn. Gee quickly woke from his sleep. Seeing all the infrared beams aimed at his body, Gee just raised both arms in the air. He didn't have to ask who it was; the bright yellow letters of the FBI and DEA were on everyone's jacket.

After reading Gee his Miranda rights, he was handcuffed and placed in the back of an FBI van. In the back of the van Gee sat back as his head was spinning non-stop. He knew that someone had to have snitched on him. And he also knew that it had to be someone that was inside his circle of drug clients. The list was long, so Gee knew that he would have to wait and be patient before the Feds released any information on the informant on the case.

Gee knew that he had to keep his cool. King had prepared him, Gotti and all the rest of his crew on what to do and expect if the Feds ever came. Number one: they had a snitch. Number two: they either had drugs, guns, or info about a murder. King told everyone to remain calm, don't say a word, ask for your lawyer, and wait to see what the charge was.

Even with all he had known Gee was still in complete shock. But no matter what he was charged and indicted for he knew that he would never snitch. He would rather die than tell on another hustler in the game. He knew and understood the consequences of his actions and being a snitch or ever working with the Feds would never happen.

Philadelphia International Airport, Southwest Philly

The American Airlines flight arrived exactly as scheduled. Plain clothed FBI agents were situated inside the terminal waiting for the two people to get off the plane. For days they had been tracking the criminals' every move. The Grand Jury had issued their indictments two days earlier. Now the FBI was here to execute it and bring their fugitives in.

When Ricardo "Killa" Gomez and Sarah "Sissy" Matthews stepped off the plane, they were quickly apprehended by FBI agents. After FBI agents had gone through all of their luggage, they found over a million dollars' worth of ecstasy pills, and a quarter of a million dollars' worth of Meth in their possession. They were both arrested and taken away without incident. Twenty minutes later, they were at the downtown FBI office, each being interrogated by agents from the Bureau.

After leaving Hahnemann Hospital, Donna and Fonz had booked a hotel room at the Holiday Inn on City Line Avenue. Fonz's gunshot wound to the leg wasn't as bad as he initially thought. The bullet had entered and exited without damaging any major arteries. Donna and Fonz had decided to lay low for a while. Gotti and Marvin were out desperately searching for any information that would lead them to the four masked culprits. Neither would rest until they found out who the man named "Ron" was, and who the other three men were.

The good news was that Fonz had another stash spot inside the house with more money and drugs hidden away. The four masked men had missed it.

"If I ever find out who robbed and shot me, they are dead!" Fonz vented. Donna didn't say a word. She was just happy to be alive. She felt blessed to still be here knowing so many others that had ended up with bullets in their heads, and grieving family members praying and crying over a casket.

Chapter 29
Three Weeks Later

For the past few weeks, Troy and his crew of masked robbers had been setting up and robbing all the top drug dealers from the tri-state area. They had taken over 40 kilos and a million dollars in cash. As for Troy, he didn't change; wasting most of his money on fast women, heavy drugs, and shopping sprees.

Inside a small motel room on Roosevelt Boulevard, Troy and Joy had just finished another round of wild sex. Now they were both sitting back on the bed snorting lines of cocaine through their burning nostrils. "Babe I want to say something to you."

"What is it?" Troy asked as he snorted a line. Joy took a deep breath and looked Troy straight in the eyes. "I think we need to slow down on the set ups and robberies. Jazzmin said she's only going to work at Nookie's, but that's it. She quit scheming because it's getting too hot. That just leaves us and your robbery crew."

"Fuck Jazzmin! She made her money and then quit on us, fuck her!" "But babe, she quit because it's getting too hot. People are noticing that every baller that comes to your father's club is getting robbed. It's becoming a pattern. Even your father said that something ain't right. I think we need to slow down before we get too caught up," Joy replied with a serious expression on her face.

Troy stood up from the bed and started pacing the floor. Suddenly, his naked body stopped in front of Joy, and he said, "Right now I just can't stop, and my crew won't stop!!"

"Why not?" Joy asked. "Because I'm broke!!" Troy said, feeling embarrassed. "What do you mean you're broke?" "I'm fucking broke Joy!! I have less than $2500 left. I been spending it all on drugs and…"

"Tricks!" Joy replied. "We need to keep setting drug dealers up! We need the money," Troy said, as he sat down beside her. Joy was speechless. She knew that Troy was now chasing after money for his drug and trick habit. And together, they were both spiraling fast downhill.

South Philly

Marvin and Gotti had the two scared men standing up facing a wall, .45 caliber pistols were aimed at their backs. "I'm going to ask you one more time. Did y'all rob me?" Gotti yelled.

"I swear it wasn't us!" one of the men said. "We was out of town." His friend added. "Then who the fuck robbed me. If it wasn't y'all then who was it?" Gotti asked.

"We don't know man! Everybody has been getting robbed!! All the top bosses in the city has been getting set up and robbed!!" one of the men said. "But it's not us!"

Gotti stood there thinking and contemplating on what to do next. He was filled with rage, especially after his sister and her boyfriend had been robbed also. He knew that someone close was behind it all. The two men against the wall were just two of many that he and Marvin ran up on.

"Get the fuck out of here!!" Gotti told them. Without any hesitation, both men turned and ran out of the alley. Marvin and Gotti both watched as they ran as fast as they could down 9th & Mifflin. As soon as they had disappeared Marvin and Gotti got back into the BMW and drove off in search of anyone with information about the robbery.

Frankford Avenue

Ski and his crazy cousin Gucci had been driving around robbing anyone with something worth taking. Ski was a known stick up boy. He still kept an eye and ear out for Gotti and Marvin. Ski knew he had to get them before they got him. Gotti had completely destroyed his street reputation. It was all over town how Gotti ran up on him and shot his friends. Ski felt like a coward, and only by killing Gotti and Marvin could he redeem himself.

"So who next?" Gucci asked. "I know some niggas that sell weed on Tioga. They out there 24-7, let's go." Ski replied. Gucci sat back, holding his loaded AK-47, and watched as Ski made a quick U-Turn and sped away.

Chapter 30
Downtown Philadelphia

Inside the Federal Prosecutor's office Darnell "Gee" Miller and his high-powered defense lawyer were seated next to each other at a large round table. Right across from them was the Federal Prosecutor, James Hightower, two FBI agents and the D.A. Candice Shaw. Gee had been escorted from his prison cell at the Federal Detention Center for an emergency meeting with the Federal and State prosecutors. So far he had refused to say a single word. King had paid top dollar for his defense team, to make sure Gee could put up a good fight.

With all the evidence stacked against him, the situation wasn't looking good. After Gee had received the discovery in his case, he learned all the names of the witnesses, police reports, drugs and the main informant that was testifying against him if he took his case to trial.

He had already sent a message through his lawyer that Sharif had been the person who set him up with the FBI.

"We know that you are a major player in the King drug organization and that you also do business with Black Gotti and his crew as well. Right now you can help yourself a great deal by cooperating and receiving a significant time reduction for any assistance that will lead to the arrest of King, Biggie, Gotti, and

Marvin. Before you answer think about your children and family. You are looking at a 20-year sentence if you take this case to trial. We have drugs, guns and several recorded incriminating conversations with you," James Hightower said.

Gee sat there with his arms folded. Looking at all the blue eyed, white faces, that stared at him. He was frustrated with himself for not seeing Sharif's betrayal, and not paying more attention to him while being blinded by the money. As the two lawyers argued back and forth, Gee sat there in total silence, letting their words fill the air. The government needed another snitch on their team; someone major on the inside that can bring the King organization crumbling down hard.

"If you agree to cooperate with us, we might be able to provide you and your family with the Federal Witness Protection Program," James said. Gee leaned over and whispered in his lawyer's ear. Seconds later, his lawyer stood up from the table and stepped away from his chair.

"First of all my client is a first-time, non-violent drug offender. His record is clean, and he is a graduate of LaSalle University. With all the new drug laws that have been passed recently, my conclusion is that he won't do more than twelve years if convicted at trial. Plus all the recordings were illegally obtained and will be thrown out because the government did not use the proper protocol to obtain recordings and the first three were wiretapped conversations. Furthermore, there is an argument for an entrapment case, because my client asked the informant on a few occasions if he was wired or trying to set him up and the informant replied no each time. So either we accept the original plea deal offer of seven years, or we go to trial and take our chances."

"I can promise you all this," he said, staring everyone in their eyes. "That the government will definitely be spending a lot of taxpayer money on this trial. So now the ball is in your court!" the lawyer said.

James Hightower let the lawyer's words sink in. He was a tough prosecutor, especially on drug dealers. He also knew that the lawyer had done his job and his case research was on point. "Okay, the seven-year deal is still on the table," the prosecutor frustratingly said. "But I can promise you this Mr. Miller, that one day we will get your friends either with or without your assistance!"

Candice Shaw sat there in silence. She was incensed but did her best to remain calm. Knowing that Gee wasn't going to break or cross his friends felt like a stab in the chest. Gee stood up dressed in an orange jumpsuit.

"I want to ask you something," he said to the prosecutor. "Yes, what's that?" he replied. "Have you ever been loyal to anything in your life?"

The prosecutor smiled and said, "Yes, my job and my family." Gee smiled and then looked him straight into his blue eyes. "Me too, my job and my family! And I will never cross them for you or anyone else! I'm no snitch!"

With that said, Gee and his lawyer were both escorted out of the conference room. Back inside the Prosecutor's James Hightower and Candice Shaw were conversing. "That son of a bitch got off too easy!" Candice shouted.

"Don't worry I'm working on a way now to charge them all under the RICO Act. If all goes well in the next few months, Gee will be re-indicted, and his crew will all be going down with him."

Candice smiled and said, "That would be perfect if you need any help from me, I'm just a phone call away. Plus I still have my own operation going on within the city. I created my drug task force a few weeks ago, so we can combine information when the time is right to get all their asses off the streets!" Candice replied.

Early the Next Day

Country strolled through the subway station at Broad and Erie and walked up the steps. He looked around and noticed the tinted black Mercedes Benz parked in front of Max's restaurant. Country ran across the street and quickly got inside. As soon as he closed the door, the car sped off.

"Wassup Country. What's the news at the club?" King asked. His midget sidekick Biggie was seated right next to him.

"Lately, there have been a number of drug dealers that have been getting robbed. Soon after they leave the club, days later we hear that four masked men had robbed them. Plus I think Troy and two of the girls are up to no good. They be whispering and having private meetings. Something is going on with them. Plus there have been some cops coming around looking for Troy and asking about him."

King paid close attention and took mental notes. After Country had finished giving him the scoop, Biggie passed him a thousand dollars and dropped him off at his house. "We will see you soon. Keep up the good work," King replied, before making a quick U-turn and driving away in the opposite direction.

Chapter 31
52nd Street
West Philly

Sissy and her partner Killa didn't hesitate at all when they were each offered a get out of jail free pass by the Federal Prosecutor. For their cooperation, they would both receive a reduction in their prison sentence. The more assistance they provided, the less time they would serve at a Federal prison. For the past two weeks, they had been working secretly with the FBI and DEA.

So far the duo had set up two drug dealers, a stolen car ring and a member of the Philly Mafia. Looking at 30-year sentences if they decided to take their case to trial, each of them agreed that cooperating was the best and only thing to do.

As they sat inside of a red Range Rover, Sissy and Killa watched as a young man ran across Market Street and got inside the car.

"Wassup y'all, everything good?" the man said. "Everything is great," Killa replied. "You got that, Pookie?" Sissy asked him. "Yeah," Pookie said, going into his jacket pocket and pulling out a large stack of hundreds. When he passed the money to Sissy, she reached under the seat and took out a bag filled with $20,000 worth of ecstasy and two new Glocks.

"Nice!" Pookie said. After the exchange was made Sissy and Killa watched as Pookie hid the guns and drugs inside his jacket and ran off. He had no idea that he had just bought drugs and guns from two FBI informants, and the wholesale was being recorded and monitored by the Feds, who were inside of a tinted Ford Taurus parked across the street.

Sissy looked over at Killa and smiled. They had successfully set up their second person of the day. "If we get them enough we won't do a damn day in prison," Sissy said before she pulled off down the street.

"We need a big fish. Someone that will only get us probation," Killa laughed. "Somebody like King or Gotti?" Sissy asked.

"Yes, exactly," Killa said as he turned up the volume on the radio. "Don't worry Killa; somebody will bite the hook."

Chapter 32
C.F.C.F.
Early the Next Morning

Gotti and Marvin sat inside of the silver BMW patiently waiting. They were both ecstatic from the recent events with Coolie's attempted murder case. After the untimely death of the police officer, the state had no choice but to drop all charges against Coolie. Without a key witness to point him out and testify against Coolie their case was sunk.

After release papers were signed Coolie walked out of the Correctional Facility a free man. After 18 long, stressful months Coolie was ready to pick up where he had left off, joining his crew and get back to the streets.

"Wassup y'all!" Coolie said, excitingly. "You my nigga!" Marvin said, giving him a handshake and a hug. Gotti embraced his cousin with a long, warm hug. He had missed him a lot, but Gotti wouldn't show too much emotion. Keeping cool was a part of his demeanor.

"Where to next? I'm free!! Let's go shopping out at King of Prussia Mall. I'm starving! Where are the bitches?" Coolie shouted. He was filled with jubilance and excitement. After spending 18 months in jail, there was nothing like being a free man. Gotti looked over at Marvin and didn't say a word. They were both quiet, watching as Coolie couldn't sit still.

Mr. Falcone sat down at the bar, watching a news segment with the District Attorney explaining her new hands-on crime plan for Philadelphia's most violent criminals. With a Cuban cigar in his mouth, he couldn't help but smile at the situation. Mr. Falcone had known the Shaw family very well. Twenty years earlier, Jack Shaw was a money making associate of his. They were good friends until Falcone had found out that Jack Shaw had been a Confidential Informant for the FBI.

A week after learning of Jack's betrayal, Falcone and a friend made an unannounced visit to the Shaw's northeast home. After shooting Jack's wife, Mr. Falcone had used a knife to savagely remove Jack's tongue, and then he cut his throat before shooting him in the head.

After the murders, Falcone and his friend ransacked the home, took some jewelry and money and made it appear as a robbery-homicide. Mr. Falcone sat at the bar with a smirk on his face, knowing that if she had walked in on them in the act 20 years ago, Candice Shaw would have been buried right next to her deceased parents.

Hilton Hotel, City Line Avenue

Donna and Fonz had continued to lay low. Together they had been brainstorming trying to come up with a list of names who they believed could've been responsible for setting them up. Fonz was still healing from the gunshot wound to his leg, so he wasn't in any shape to go see Gotti to plan his revenge on his attackers. And besides, he still wasn't completely sure who the responsible people were. All they had was the name Ron and a pair of green eyes.

"I just hung up with my brother. My cousin Coolie got out of jail this morning," Donna said with a smile on her beautiful face.

"That's wassup," Fonz replied in a calm demeanor. "What's wrong babe?" Donna said as she laid her head on his chest.

"I'm just so upset with myself for putting you in so much danger and getting you caught up in all my shit." Donna kissed Fonz on the lips and said, "We are in this together babe. It could've happened to anyone. You just have to be more cautious the next time. The drug game is full of crooks, snakes, and haters that want to take what others have earned. Don't worry; my brother will find out who's behind it all. I gave him our list of names and he knows about Ron and his green eyes. So just let your leg heal and stay focused until we get us another place to live."

Fonz's face finally showed a smile and a small glimpse of hope. He loved Donna with every muscle in his body, and there was nothing he wouldn't do for her happiness.

Philadelphia International Airport

Coolie looked at Gotti and Marvin and saw their serious expression. "Wassup fellas?" he asked. "Why are we at the airport?"

Gotti pulled over and parked the car and everyone got out. "Damn, wassup? Coolie asked. Somebody say something," he said.

With the key, Gotti popped open the trunk, and he and Marvin took out two suitcases. "Everything you need is inside the suitcases. New clothes, shoes, a new ID, driver's license, passport and $25,000 in cash," Gotti replied.

"Are you serious Gotti?" "Yes Coolie, I'm sending you down to Atlanta. You can't stay up here. You're a wanted man! The cops will kill you on sight! They think you're a cop killer! If you stay around you will just bring a lot of unnecessary heat on us, and we already got the Feds and other people on our backs watching our every move!"

"But I'm your cousin! I have always had your back. Both of y'all backs!" Coolie said with sadness in his voice. Gotti placed his arm around his cousin's shoulder and said, "I appreciate all that you have done for me, but right now your safety is all I care about. You stood strong on the case, now please let me stand strong for you. When shit calms down, I will call you, but until then you need to get as far away from Philly as possible!" Gotti told him. "I love you cuz, just trust me on this," he added.

Coolie looked at the seriousness in both of their eyes and knew deep down that what Gotti was telling him to do was the right thing. Philly was hot!!

"If you need more money just call Donna and I will have it sent to you," Gotti said. "She knows too?" Coolie asked.

"Yes, she knows, I told her." Coolie shook his head then grabbed the two suitcases. Without saying goodbye or giving them a hug he turned and walked away. Gotti and Marvin watched as Coolie walked through the crowded airport terminal towards American Airlines. When he had disappeared from sight, Gotti and Marvin got back into the car and drove away without saying a single word.

Chapter 33

Big Nook and Tori sat inside his office counting the week's profits. Over $40,000 was laid out on a small table. Jazzmin and Joy were running the bar, while Country was keeping an eye on the front door. After counting up the money Big Nook opened the safe and placed the money inside with all of the rest of his cash. He stocked up on bottles of liquor, wine, and vodka, for all the big time ballers that were scheduled to visit the club this week. He also paid off the local cops for the rest of the month so everything would go smoothly.

While Big Nook and Tori were talking Troy knocked on the door and walked into the office. "Wassup Dad, I got your text?" Troy said. "I need you to do me a favor and run Joy to the store to pick up some supplies. Troy smiled and said, "Sure Dad, no problem. Whatever you need I got you."

"Are you sure King?" Gotti said into the cell phone. "I'm positive. I will text you the address right now. Just make sure you and Marvin go handle that," King replied.

"Don't worry, we on it," Gotti said before he ended the call. "Wassup?" Marvin asked. Gotti shook his head and said, "You're not going to believe this!"

Marvin was all ears as he listened to Gotti tell him all about the news he had just gotten from King.

Marvin couldn't believe it, but both men knew that King's word was gospel.

"You ready to go take care of this problem?" Loading up his 9mm, "with pleasure," Marvin smirked. Gotti made a quick U-turn and drove towards the small, suburban town of Cheltenham, Pennsylvania.

Parked in the back of an old warehouse, Troy had his hands behind his head enjoying the pleasing sensation of Joy's amazing blowjob. Joy was so good at oral sex that in less than three minutes Troy could feel the oncoming orgasm already forming inside his trembling body. As Joy slid her mouth up and down his dick, Troy exploded inside her warm, wet mouth. "Ahhh! Oh my god!" he yelled out. "Now let's hurry up before Nook calls," Joy smiled.

~~~

Inside the privacy of her Mt. Erie home, Candice Shaw sat down on the sofa and opened a small briefcase. She reached inside and grabbed a brown folder. Candice sat back and began reading through all the papers inside. The secret file held information about the murder of her parents. For years she had been gathering more and more information about their case.

Even though there had been no clues or evidence left behind by the murderers, she had a gut feeling about the person she felt was responsible. Her father had been a major associated with the Italian Mafia, and through thorough research she had learned that he was also an FBI informant, working secretly to take down the boss Joseph Falcone.

After reading through all her notes, Candice pulled out a small photo of Mr. Falcone and stared at it. "You are going down for what you did to my parents!! You and every member of your crew will one day feel my wrath," she said, before placing the photo back inside the folder.

South Philly

Sitting inside his dark blue Cadillac Escalade, Mr. Falcone was talking to his right-hand man and mob underboss Vincent Costello. "Did you take care of that problem?" Mr. Falcone asked him.

"Yes boss, he's sleeping with the fishes." "Good, he was a rat, and all rats should be fed to the sharks," Mr. Falcone said.

"Vinny we have to continue to keep our circle small and tight. We can't afford to slip up again and allow another rat to sneak into our crew."

"Don't worry boss; I'm on it. If there's a rat, I will find him and exterminate him for you. My father and three of my uncles are all serving life sentences in Club Fed because of rats!! They have no honor, and they all need to be disposed of," Vinny said.

Mr. Falcone smiled and nodded his head. For over ten years he and Vinny had run the Philly mob with an iron fist. They had only trusted each other. Each knew that the game was cruel, and trust was hard to find.

Later That Night

Coolie walked into his plush downtown Atlanta apartment and sat down on the leather sofa. He was very upset that he had been forced to leave Philly, the only city he had ever known. A few times he had thought about disobeying Gotti's request and going back home, but he knew that it wouldn't be wise and Gotti would be pissed off if he did return.

An hour later, Coolie was searching for a companion on Backpages. The only thing that could relieve his stressful day was a night of sex. Hearing the knock at the door startled Coolie and he jumped up from the sofa. He walked over and looked through the small peep hole. When he saw the beautiful woman on the other side of the door, he quickly opened it and let her inside.

In walked one of the most beautiful, dark skinned women that Coolie had ever laid his eyes on. "Hi Philly, I'm Meeka," she said in her Southern accent. Coolie smiled. He couldn't keep his eyes off of her. Meeka was a dark chocolate beauty, with an hourglass figure on her 5 foot 5-inch frame. She had dark brown eyes, high cheekbones with finely trimmed eyebrows, plus she had a round fat ass that stopped traffic.

"How much?" "$100 an hour, Philly," she said, showing her beautiful, white teeth. Coolie passed her ten one hundred dollar bills and said, "Well get relaxed, I want you to stay till the morning if you don't mind."

Meeka took the money and said, "I don't mind at all." Meeka liked what she saw in Coolie. He was tall, light skinned and very handsome. Plus he had a Philly accent that turned her on.

"You smoke?" Coolie asked. "Yeah, I blow and drink a little too," Meeka replied. "Cool, then get relaxed, we got all night."

Meeka took off her jacket and shoes and sat down on the sofa next to Coolie. They rolled up a blunt, laced with some loud marijuana and smoked while they talked. The attraction was mutual and strong, and neither of them could wait until the smoke session was over and the sex session could begin.

Chapter 34
Cheltenham Township

Cheltenham Township is a small, suburban town on the outskirts of Philadelphia. It mostly consisted of middle-class families that had moved from the rough, violent streets in urban Philly. Not too far from the Cheltenham Mall, the Feds had their number one street informant, hidden safely away. Sharif was due to testify on a major cocaine trafficker from West Philly named Manny. He had to be in court at 10 AM, the next morning.

~~~

For forty-five minutes, Gotti and Marvin had been parked across the street from the home. It was pitch black, and no one was out on this cold, winter night. They watched as two shadowy figures walked throughout the house then finally went upstairs. As soon as the two people went upstairs, Gotti and Marvin exited the car, carrying loaded 9 mm's with attached silencers. They walked around the back of the two-story home and approached the back door.

Marvin used a small screwdriver to jam the lock on the door. With little resistance, the locked door suddenly popped open. With guns aimed they tiptoed through the house and headed upstairs. As they crept up the stairs, they could hear the sound of voices coming from the front room. With each step, the voices grew louder.

When they finally approached the back room, Gotti took a deep breath and then kicked the door in with all his force. With stunned looks on their faces, he and Marvin couldn't believe their eyes. Sharif was lying across the bed totally naked. His arms were handcuffed behind his back, and his friend Mike was lying on top of him fucking Sharif in the ass. The two snitches were also undercover homosexuals. They had been secret lovers for years.

Sharif and Mike both jumped up in fear. "Y'all fucking rat faggots!!" Gotti shouted. "Please God don't kill us!" Sharif begged. "Shut up you faggot!" Marvin said. Sharif and Mike sat on the bed with the look of pure fear on their faces.

"There are two things that I hate more than anything in this world," Gotti said, as he aimed his pistol at Sharif's head. "A rat and a fucking faggot!" Then without hesitation, Gotti and Marvin both unloaded their guns into the heads and torsos of Sharif and Mike's naked bodies. They watched as the two corpses slumped on the bed, instantly filling it with a pool of dark, red blood.

Before leaving the house they wiped off everything they touched, eliminating any clues or fingerprints. Then Gotti snapped a picture of the horrific scene and texted it to King. Five minutes later, they were both inside the car headed back to Philly.

"Oh my god! Yes Daddy, beat this pussy up Philly!" Meeka shouted out in ecstasy. Coolie had Meeka pinned down to the bed, with her legs behind her neck, fucking her rough and hard. The dick was so good that Meeka couldn't stop coming. Coolie watched as her eyes rolled to the back of her head and she continued to scream and call on God. Then suddenly her body began to tremble and shake. The more she screamed and shook the more it turned Coolie on.

Suddenly a gush of liquid squirted out of Meeka's pussy. Coolie paid it no attention as he continued to fuck Meeka like it was the last piece of pussy on earth. Meeka was on Cloud 20; she had never been fucked this good in all her life.

Coolie turned her around and started fucking Meeka from behind, touching spots that she had never knew existed before. Tears of joy ran from her eyes as her breathing got more and more intense.

"Oh, my! Oh my god! Damn baby! You so deep!!" Meeka shouted. "Whose pussy is this?" Coolie asked. "Whose pussy is this?"

"Yours Philly! It's all yours Philly!" she yelled. For the next few hours, Coolie fucked Meeka with all the energy in his body. After 18 long months of being locked up with niggas he had been long overdue for some sexual healing. And tonight Meeka would feel every single day he spent behind those prison bars.

Chapter 35
2:45 AM
Broad & Lehigh

The four masked men had been patiently waiting and watching. Troy had given them all the info they needed to complete the new task. They each exited the stolen van and walked across the dimly lit street. Two of the masked men walked around back and the other two walked up to the front door.

After smashing in the front door, they ran into the house with guns blazing. At the same time, the other two masked men kicked in the back door and did the same thing. Inside the master bedroom was one of the top heroin dealers in the city. His name was Ramon Jackson. He was in bed lying next to his beautiful wife, Tina. Their two daughters were inside their own bedroom, being tied up and duct taped.

Ramon Jackson was a heroin kingpin. He had over 40 workers and businesses all over the tri-state area. Two days before, he and his wife had visited Big Nook's Afterhour Club. It was a decision that would cost him.

After emptying the safe behind the bed, the four masked men ran out of the house, leaving the entire family tied up and duct taped in their rooms. Ramon and his wife had been pistol whipped until they fell unconscious. Twenty minutes later, Ramon had awakened with blurry vision and a severe headache.

His wife Tina wasn't as lucky; she died from the blunt force trauma to her head.

Early the Next Morning

FBI tacticians were walking around the house searching for any clues that could help solve the double homicide of Sharif and Mike. The one thing they knew was that someone on the inside had disclosed information on the whereabouts of their two informants. Sharif's murder was a major setback for the FBI and DEA. He was set to testify against a major drug dealer and two more later in the week. His untimely death would surely put a halt to their major drug cases. Top FBI officials planned to do a major internal investigation. They were determined to find the mole.

Black and two of his goons walked into Kirby's Barbershop and slammed the door behind him. No one said anything to Black and his crew. The word on the streets was that he had been robbed and beaten at his Southwest stash house.

Black looked around at all the scared faces and shouted out, "Tell Gotti that Black is looking for him!!" Then just like that he and his two goons strolled out of the barbershop. After getting back into his car he and his crew headed to the Crab House on Germantown Avenue, another popular spot, to let more people know that he was looking for Gotti and Marvin. Black knew that there would be consequences for his actions and threats, but he wasn't afraid of Gotti's killer reputation on the streets. He was a killer too, and fear was something he didn't do well.

~~~

On the opposite side of town Ski and Gucci were driving around searching for Gotti and Marvin too, but unlike Black, they didn't want anyone to know that they were driving around on a personal manhunt. Ski's reason to kill Gotti was strictly out of fear and embarrassment. He knew that if he didn't climinate Gotti and Marvin that they would surely one day kill him. Now, he was the prey on a serious mission to kill the predators.

"Let's go down South Philly and see if anyone down there has heard or seen Gotti's bitch ass," Ski said. "We out," Gucci said, driving down Broad Street.

Atlanta, GA

Coolie and Meeka had just finished another round of hard, passionate sex. They had been at it for two days straight. "So what now babe?" Meeka said, laying across Coolie's chest. "You're done with me after beating my pussy up for two days?"

Coolie smiled, as he ran his hand through her hair. "Who said that I was done with you?" Coolie sat up and replied.

Meeka smiled. In just the short time that they had met each was feeling the other. It was the best sex that either had ever had. "I'm just saying what are we gonna do now? Will I see you again? Or you got what you paid for, and now you're done with me?" Meeka said, with seriousness in her voice.

Coolie smiled and said, "I'm definitely not done with you. I want you to be mine." Meeka's eyes popped open and she said, "You do? Seriously is that what you want?"

"Yes, I'm serious. I like your sexy chocolate ass!" Coolie replied. "Don't play with me Philly!!" "I'm serious Meeka. If I wasn't I wouldn't have said it."

Meeka smiled and said, "Ok, but you still have a lot to find out about me. I'm damaged goods." "We all are damaged goods!!!" Coolie replied.

Meeka looked Coolie straight into his eyes and said, "Just promise me that you won't hurt me. Trust me I've been hurt too many times."

"I'm not going to hurt you, just always keep it 100% with me and we good!" "I'm gonna do better than that; I'm gonna keep it 1000%!" Meeka said, as she leaned over and kissed Coolie on his lips.

~~~

On the corner of 4th & South Street, King and Biggie were sitting inside a tinted Mercedes. They watched as beautiful women of all races walked up and down the crowded, boisterous street. South Street is one of the most popular locations in Philly. Clothing stores, restaurants, and bars all lined both sides of the street.

Ten minutes later, a tall, slim white man approached the passenger side window and tapped on the glass. Biggie rolled down the tinted window and passed the man a yellow envelope. Inside the envelope was $10,000 in cash. No words were said, as King and Biggie watched as the man calmly walked away, disappearing into the crowd of people.

"Call Gotti and tell him about the other two rats," King said before he started the car and drove off. "Ok," Biggie replied.

Chapter 36
Four Days Later

"Are you okay babe?" Tori asked Gotti, after seeing the serious expression on his face. "I'm good babe, I just have a busy day ahead of me," he replied.

"Do you need me for anything?" Tori asked, as she walked over and sat on the sofa beside him. "Naw babe, I'm good. Me and Marvin will take care of everything."

Tori knew her man better than anyone. She could tell when something serious was weighing heavy on his mind. "I heard about Sharif and his friend. I saw it on the news," she said.

Gotti looked Tori straight into her eyes and smiled then he said, "Well, one thing is for sure, he won't be coming back into your father's club disrespecting you anymore!"

"How did you know that?" Tori replied. "I got ears and eyes everywhere," he grinned. Tori didn't respond. She knew that Gotti had been involved with Sharif's murder in some type of way. They never liked each other, and everyone knew it. "Lay back baby, let me help relieve some stress before you hit the streets," she said.

Gotti watched as Tori pulled down his pants and boxers and began kissing and sucking on his hard dick. Less than ten minutes later, he was trembling beneath her, exploding inside of her warm, wet mouth.

Downtown Philadelphia

Inside the Federal Prosecutor's office, James Hightower, his assistant Roy Carter and Philadelphia District Attorney Candice Shaw were all talking.

"We have a mole inside one of our offices," James said. "There's no way in the world Sharif's whereabouts should have been known. Only a few individuals knew about it."

"Well I can assure you that no one from my office or staff said a single word," Candice replied. "We just have to be more cautious and not allow this incident to ever happen again," Roy said.

"We were really counting on Sharif's testimony in a few major cases," James said. "Don't worry, we got informants lining up to make deals," Roy said. "Yes we do, but Sharif was the most valuable informant we had in a long time. It's an embarrassment to both of our offices that a government informant was murdered inside a secret safe house. That was uncalled for, and we need an immediate investigation done to find out who the leak is," James replied.

Donna sat down next to Fonz and said, "Babe, can I ask you something?" Fonz looked at her and replied, "Yes, what is it?" "Do you think Troy had something to do with us getting robbed?"

"I thought about it, but it was four guys, and I don't think Troy has the heart or smarts to put something together like that. I don't trust him, never did, but I don't believe he's behind it," Fonz replied.

"Well, I'm just saying, as soon as you start getting drugs from him you get set up and robbed by four masked men. It could be a coincidence, but I still don't trust him at all. He is a snake, and snakes bite anything and everything."

Fonz sat there letting the words sink in. He knew that Troy couldn't be trusted, but he didn't want to believe that he was a part of the crew that robbed and shot him.

West Philly, Later that Night

Big Nook looked around at his crowded club with a huge smile on his face. Ballers, hustlers and drug dealers of all races were spending money on food and bottles like it had grown on trees and the big spending gamblers were on the craps and card tables. Behind the bar, Tori, Jazzmin, and Joy were serving and flirting with the high rollers.

In the back of the room, Troy watched from a distance. He had been quietly observing everyone inside the club. Troy started walking around the club typing notes into his iPhone. He was desperate for some cash because he had spent most of his own on drugs and women. From behind the bar, Jazzmin watched Troy maneuver through the crowd. She knew what he was up to, and deep inside her, his secret was eating her alive.

Chapter 37
Two Days Later

"Hello?" Donna said, answering her cell phone. "Hey Donna, it's me Rock down at the barbershop on 26th and Ridge Avenue."

"Wassup Rock?" Donna asked as she sat up on the bed. "I'm just calling to let you know that some guy Black and a few of his goons have been coming around the shop asking questions and looking for your brother."

"Are you serious?" Donna said in a surprised voice. "Yes, I'm dead serious. And I also heard that Ski, the stick-up boy has been asking about Gotti as well."

"Thank you Rock, I really appreciate this; I'll let my brother know what you told me," Donna said, before ending the call.

"What was that all about?" Fonz asked. "That was Rock from the barbershop. We went to high school together. He just told me that a few guys have been going around asking about my brother," Donna said, as she started texting Gotti the names Rock had given her

"Will Gotti be safe out there?" Fonz asked. "Gotti knows the streets better than anyone! But he will still need some backup for all of these niggas that are asking about him. I'm sure they are up to no good. Who knows what my brother did to them."

"So what do you want to do about it?" Fonz asked. "I know exactly what I'm going to do," Donna said, texting someone with her cell phone.

West Philly, 41st and Lancaster Avenue

Inside a small house, Troy was venting out his anger to the four men seated at the table. "We have to do it! Just don't hurt anyone!" he shouted.

"Are you sure man?" one of the men said. "Yes, it will be simple and fast, plus he has over a million dollars stashed away! I'm fucking broke! I need money now!!!"

"Okay, we will hit him tomorrow night, but I hope this shit don't backfire on us," another one of the men said.

"And remember, no one gets hurt," Troy said, before walking out of the house. The four men looked around at each other and just shook their heads.

"After the next robbery, he has to go," one of them said. "Yeah, he is a loose cannon." Troy walked over to the parked Gold Lexus and got inside where Joy was patiently waiting for him. The first thing she noticed was the desperate look on his face. Each time Troy made a bad decision, he had the same look. She saw it too many times. "Is everything ok?" she asked.

"No! I'm fucking broke! I need money!" he snapped. "Didn't you and your friends just discuss that?" Joy said, starting up the car and pulling off down the street.

"They are not my friends! I honestly can't stand any of them, especially Ron's ass! It's just business, nothing less, nothing more!" Troy said, as he went into the glove compartment and took out a small, glass pipe.

"Babe, I thought you said you were going to stop that," Joy said. "I need a hit girl, just drive back to the club and mind your damn business." Joy kept silent and watched as Troy placed a small rock of crack cocaine into the pipe and then flicked on his lighter. She drove, watching as Troy inhaled and exhaled the potent drug into his yearning system.

"I'm a fuck up! A total fuck up. But I have to do what I have to do. And right now money is my only option," Troy said.

~~~

Meeka had driven Coolie all over the city. She had shown him all of the hottest, most popular spots in Atlanta. Both of them were smitten with the other. Meeka was so infatuated with her new Philly lover that she had quit her late night call girl job and was now working as a receptionist at a downtown office building.

Though Coolie was happy at the moment, he still couldn't help but miss his Philly hometown. He was homesick beyond words. "I need a big favor babe."

"Anything for you Daddy," Meeka replied as she pulled over and parked the car. "Anything?" Coolie replied with a smile.

Meeka reached over and started unzipping his jeans. "Anything you need."

Chapter 38
11:23 PM
12th & Market Street

Parked right outside of the famous Hard Rock Café, Gotti and Marvin had been patiently waiting. After receiving some valuable information from King, they had set out to finish a very important mission. Forty minutes later, they watched as a man and woman walked out of the front entrance door. The two of them then got inside of a black truck and slowly pulled away down the dark street.

Gotti and Marvin pulled off behind them, staying a few cars away to avoid being noticed. They followed the truck into a new home development on Ridge Avenue. The sky was pitched black, and not a single soul was outside. Gotti and Marvin had their loaded 9mm pistols clutched in their arms. Each gun had an attached silencer screwed on it.

When the truck pulled up in front of a new two story home and parked, Gotti and Marvin slowly pulled up a few spots away. The tinted Impala they were in protected them from being seen. As soon as the two people opened the doors and stepped out of the truck, Gotti and Marvin opened the doors and quickly rushed towards them. They were caught completely off guard.

"Take what you want!!" the female said in a frightened voice. "Okay, I want your life!" Gotti replied before he and Marvin fired their guns and unloaded every bullet into their heads and chest. They watched as the two bodies slumped hard to the ground.

Less than five minutes later, Gotti and Marvin were driving back down Ridge Avenue. Gotti then took out his cell phone and called a private number. He wasn't worried about being heard on the phone by FBI wiretaps because all the cell phones they used were pre-programmed by his friend Roscoe to avoid Federal bugs.

"Talk to me," King answered. "The rats are both stinking in their driveway!" Gotti replied. King smiled and said, "Good shit! Sissy and Killa were on the Fed's payroll. On a mission to take us all down."

"Well the Feds are going to need two more to take their place," Gotti laughed.

Chapter 39
South Philly

"The whole game is fucked up and full of rats!" Mr. Falcone yelled out at a group of Italian men. "Rats! Rats! Rats!" Mr. Falcone had just received news that two of his friends had just been indicted, after being set up by FBI informants. The group of men all stood around watching and listening as Mr. Falcone continued to vent out his anger and hatred for government informants.

"There are no more stand up men! Everyone sees the money and fame, but no one understands that with the joy comes the pain...The cops, the Feds, prison, and death. When the shit hits the fan, who is willing to stand?"

Mr. Falcone walked around the room smoking a Cuban cigar. He stared at each man and then stopped in his tracks.

"If anyone in my circle is ever found to be a rat, I promise you I will personally cut your dick off and stick it down your throat after I put a bullet in the middle of your head! Then I will kill everyone you love."

With that said Mr. Falcone walked out of the room, leaving the group of men in total shock. After walking out to his car he got inside and drove off down the dark street. Unbeknownst to Mr. Falcone, an undercover FBI surveillance team had been watching him and his crew for months. And all the conversations inside of his social club had been secretly recorded.

    Mr. Falcone didn't know that a rat had been in his own crew and he had been incriminating himself many times over. Every day he would discuss murder and robbery plots to his associates, and each conversation had been recorded on an FBI wire.

    The Feds had known almost everything that Mr. Falcone and his crew were involved in. Candice Shaw had put his name on the top of her list and had given the Feds all the info she had gathered over the years. She knew that Mr. Falcone was somehow involved in her parents' murders. Now with the help of the Federal Government Candice Shaw would not rest until her parents' murderer was locked up for life.

Chapter 40
The Next Day
Germantown Avenue

Inside Tymeka's Soul Food Restaurant, Black and one of his goons were sitting at a small table eating their chicken platters and talking about how they wanted to kill Gotti and take over Gotti's drug organization. They had no idea that they were being overheard by one of Gotti's female cousins that worked at the restaurant. As they continued to eat and discuss their ruthless plans, the woman walked to the back of the restaurant and texted Gotti's sister Donna.

~~~

"What the hell is going on?" Federal Prosecutor James Hightower vented. "How did two more of our Federal informants get murdered in cold blood?"

His assistant Roy Carter and Candice Shaw both looked on with bemused expressions. No one had a word to say. "Sissy and Killa were both vital to some major cases!! Now I have to hold back on a few indictments that were all set to go out this week. This is not good, and I am going to get down to the bottom of this!! Roy, I want an internal sweep of the entire department! I want names of all the agents that are assigned to Sissy and Killa's cases!"

"Okay sir, I'm on it," Roy said before he stormed out of the office. "Someone is going around killing our informants! And they are getting crucial info from someone on the inside," James said.

"Well, I can assure you that it is no one in the D.A.'s office. I run a tight ship," Candice replied. James stood up from his chair and began to pace back and forth across the room. He was furious, and Candice could see it plastered all over his pale face.

"I am going to find out who the mole is. And when I do he will be prosecuted to the fullest extent!!" Candice sat in her chair quietly. She knew James meant every word he said.

Germantown Avenue

The tinted black van had been parked right outside the restaurant for a half hour. The two masked men inside were each holding fully loaded Uzi submachine guns. They patiently watched as Black and his friend finished eating their food and stood up from the table. After paying the bill, they exited the restaurant and walked across the street to their car. Without hesitation, the two masked men jumped out of the van with guns aimed at Black and his friend's head.

"Do something stupid and y'all will die right here!" one of the men said. Black stood there shaking his head in total disbelief. He had been caught slipping and outgunned.

"Fuck dat!" his friend said as he reached for his gun under his shirt. Before he could reach it the submachine gun was ripping through his tall, frail body. When it was over, he laid dead on the ground with over 30 bullet holes in his body.

"Get the fuck in the van!" they told Black. Seeing what had just happened to his friend Black did as he was told and stepped into the van. While one of the men drove off the other one sat back with his gun pointed at his head.

"Where y'all taking me?" Black asked with fear written all over his face. "To the doctor's office." Black sat back in total silence and in complete fear of his life. He knew that he had made a big mistake by going around the city talking dirty about Gotti and Marvin.

"I know y'all are doing this for Gotti. Whatever he's paying y'all, I will double it. Just don't kill me. I have a daughter," Black said, as he started to tremble uncontrollably. The masked man didn't respond. He just sat there with his hand on the trigger as the other masked man headed to West Philly.

Chapter 41
Nookie's Afterhours Club

Everyone inside the popular late night spot was enjoying themselves. Drug dealers, hustlers, and ballers from as far as Atlanta were all inside gambling, drinking and partying. Big Nook stood near the bar watching an intense pool game between two major drug dealer. They were betting a thousand dollars a game. The three bartenders were all behind the bar serving drinks and flirting with the paying customers, while Troy was standing on a back wall talking to Country while looking up at the clock on the wall.

Suddenly the front door was kicked in, and four masked gunmen rushed through the door yelling and pointing loaded guns. "Everyone get the fuck down on the ground!!!" one of the men yelled out. With shocked looks on their faces, everyone did as they were told, while three of the men ran around the club going inside of people's pockets, and taking money off of card tables. One of the men ordered Big Nook to walk back to his office.

"Just give them what they want Dad!" Troy yelled out. Jazzmin laid on the ground shaking her head, knowing that Troy was the one behind it all. "How could he rob his own father?" she thought to herself.

Moments later, the masked man rushed out of Big Nook's office carrying a duffle bag filled with cash. "Are we good fellas?" he asked his crew. "Not yet," the masked man with the piercing green eyes said.

Everyone inside the club lay still in total fear as they watched the man walk over to Troy aiming his weapon. "What's going on?" Troy shouted. "Die, you fucking snake!!" the man said before he pulled the trigger of his 9mm and unloaded the whole clip into Troy's head and body. Tori and the other women inside the club started screaming. In less than five minutes, the four men had robbed Big Nook's club for over a million dollars in jewels and cash, leaving just one casualty in their wake of terror.

Back inside the stolen van, the four men were all excited about the robbery. "Troy had to go; he was weak. Plus he would've eventually fucked up and taken us all down. Anyone that's willing to set up and rob his own father needs to be dead."

All the men nodded in agreement. "Now let's go back to the stash spot and split this money up," one of the men said.

Inside Big Nook's, a stunned crowd stood around Troy's corpse. "No! No!" Tori continued to scream out and cry. Country, Jazzmin, Joy and Big Nook all stood around with shocked expressions. After the ambulance had come and taken away Troy's body, police and detectives had to question Big Nook and all the employees at the club. All the customers left right after the robbers had disappeared. No one wanted to be around when the cops arrived.

As the detectives questioned everyone, no one was more distressed than Joy. The tears fell from her eyes like a waterfall as she sobbed the whole time. After being questioned Big Nook locked up the club and he, Joy and Tori drove to the University of Pennsylvania Hospital. When they got there Troy's death was confirmed. He had been shot multiple times in the head and chest, death was inevitable.

Back inside her car Jazzmin sat back crying and confused. "Why did they kill Troy?" she thought. All she could do was scratch her head with questions. "Was he a liability? Was he going to rat them out?" Jazzmin thought. All she knew was that something went wrong and Troy ended up on the wrong side of a bullet. Jazzmin was now scared for her life. She knew everything. Things that would get her killed.

Chapter 42

Randy "Doc" Patterson was cold blooded and heartless. He was a psychopathic, maniac, suffering from a chronic mental disorder and violent social behavior. He was also a member of the Black Scarface – King Drug Cartel. Mostly used to dismember bodies and slowly torture their enemies. Doc was a tall, slim white man that lived in a hood surrounded by blacks. He stood out like a sore thumb, but he had lived there so long he had been accepted as one of their own. He also never did anything to be under suspicion. Doc was quiet and very reclusive. Only a few had known about his darkest and most disturbing secrets. A year earlier King had introduced Gotti to Doc. So far Gotti had used his services twice. He had been pleased with the results both times.

"What's going on?" Black shouted as he laid totally naked on a wooden table. Doc walked over, and duct taped Black's mouth shut. He looked down at Black's tied-up naked body and smirked. He was very pleased with the sight of his new piece of fresh meat.

"Thanks, Gotti, I will take care of this problem for y'all." Gotti and Marvin stood back and watched as Doc stuck a long, syringe into Black's neck. Seconds later, Black's entire body felt numb, but he was still conscious of everything that was going on around him. Then Doc began to undress himself and climb on top of Black's body.

"What are you about to do?" Gotti asked with a confused look on his face. Doc smiled and said, "I'm about to fuck him," he answered before swallowing a Viagra. "Then I'm going to eat his eyes, ears, tongue, fingers and toes. Then..."

"That's enough," Marvin said, with a disgusted look on his face. "Do you Doc, and just call me when you're done," Gotti said, before he and Marvin walked out of the basement.

"That dude is sick!" Gotti said, as he looked at all the missed calls from Tori.

Chapter 43
Three Days Later

Roscoe was sitting at his desk on his computer waiting for Gotti and Marvin to come to his house. He had discovered some very crucial information and needed to tell them about it as soon as possible. Moments later, Gotti and Marvin walked inside with serious expressions on their faces.

"What's so important Roscoe?" Gotti asked. Roscoe straightened his glasses and sat up in his chair. "Last night I successfully hacked into the Philadelphia Police and D.A. Office computer systems and discovered some vital information."

"What is it?" Marvin asked. Roscoe started to type on the computer and seconds later the District Attorney secret indictment list appeared on the screen. On the list were ten names of men and women that had been secretly indicted by the Grand Jury. When Gotti saw his father's name on the list and a few other people he knew he just stood there shaking his head.

"In many cases, a secret indictment made by the Grand Jury, formally charging the accused of a crime, is kept sealed until the accused has been arrested," Roscoe said. "I know, now I need to call my father and tell him what I've learned," Gotti replied.

"I thought you couldn't stand your father," Marvin asked. "I can't stand the old man, but I can't stand cops even more!"

Roscoe watched as Gotti and Marvin rushed out the door and got back inside the waiting black Range Rover that was parked right outside. "Before we meet up with my father we need to go make another stop and go check up on Doc," Gotti said.

Marvin looked over at Gotti and said, "Man, I'm not sure my stomach is up to seeing that crazy dude. He really freaks me out."

Gotti laughed and said, "Marvin, let me find out that a nigga like you is scared of some old white dude."

Chapter 44
Twenty Minutes Later

Gotti and Marvin pulled up and parked across the street from Doc's West Philly home. After knocking on the door, Doc greeted them with a big smile. "Hey fellas, it's good to see y'all again. I think y'all will both be pleased with what I've done with the victim," he said, walking back to the small kitchen.

When the three men entered the kitchen, Gotti and Marvin noticed two large pots boiling on the stove. On the kitchen table was thirty small clear Ziplock bags with what appeared to be some type of cooked meat inside.

"What's that?" Marvin asked. Doc grinned and started laughing. "That's your friend Black." Gotti and Marvin stood back in complete silence. Then Doc walked over to the freezer and opened it. He reached down and pulled out a large, plastic bag with Black's head inside. The tongue, eyes, nose and ears were all missing.

"He was delicious," Doc said. Marvin was so disturbed that he turned and walked back into the other room. "What's all the Ziplock bags for?" Gotti asked.

"The homeless. I've been cooking Black's flesh and feeding it to the homeless. They think it's chicken or beef, so they don't care," Doc replied with a smirk. I will dispose of the head and everything else I don't use in the Schuylkill River when I'm done."

Gotti just nodded his head. He knew Doc was a cold-blooded lunatic and it was best to be his friend rather than his enemy. "Try a bag," Doc said. "Naw, I'm good." "You will be surprised how good it tastes," Doc added.

"I'm a vegetarian," Gotti lied, as he shook Doc's hand and walked away to go join Marvin. When they got back inside the Range Rover, neither man had said a word. But both men had disturbed looks on their faces as they headed to South Philly.

Chapter 45
Northeast Philly

"What's wrong with you Joy?" Big Nook asked, seeing the sad look on her face. "You have been very distant the past few days." Since the death of Troy, Joy had been very quiet and spent most of her time alone.

"I'm fine," Joy replied. Big Nook walked over and grabbed Joy's hands. "I know that you are very upset and saddened by my son's death, but all we can do now is pray that Troy is in a much better place. The funeral is in a few days. I'm gonna need you to get yourself together. You've been taking Troy's death harder than me and his sister."

"It just bothered me the way he was gunned down," Joy said. Big Nook gave Joy a hug and held her tight in his arms. "Don't worry; I'm gonna find out who the responsible people were. I have my men on the streets searching for answers," he said, trying his best to comfort her.

Big Nook had no idea that Joy knew exactly who was responsible. She knew everything because she had been a part of all the robberies that Troy had planned and plotted. Still, she couldn't say a word because Big Nook would find out about their secret affair and all of the robberies of the people at his club. Joy was caught between a rock and a hard place. The man she was in love with was dead and gone, and she knew the killers who were responsible for his murder. Besides, that Joy was in a relationship with her former lover's father; a man that she didn't love at all.

"I'll be back a Lil' later; I have to go get Tori so we can get all the funeral arrangements in order." "Okay," Joy said, as she watched Big Nook walk out the front door. As soon as Big Nook got inside his truck and drove off Joy burst out in a flow of tears. All she could think about was Troy.

Chapter 46
South Philly

At a secret location near Broad and Snyder Avenue Gotti, Marvin and his father Joseph Falcone were inside the kitchen talking. Gotti had told his father everything that he had learned about his secret indictment.

"Are you sure about this?" Mr. Falcone asked once again. "I'm positive. Your name is on the list and they are planning on arresting you very soon."

"Did it say what I'm being indicted for?" "Drugs, racketeering, extortion, and murder. Someone in your organization is a rat. Someone has been wearing a wire, and I'm pretty sure that your place is under heavy surveillance. They only issue an indictment if they got some vital info to take you down," Gotti said.

Mr. Falcone stood up from his chair and just shook his head. He was frustrated beyond words. "It's that bitch, Candice Shaw! That piece of shit has been trying to lock me up for years!! But I'm not going back to prison. They got 15 years out of me the first time, and they won't get another day."

"So what are you going to do?" Gotti asked. "I'm leaving town. But first I have some loose ends to tie up," Mr. Falcone said, as the three men put on their coats and left the house.

After Gotti and Marvin drove off Mr. Falcone called someone on his cell phone. "Hello boss, wassup?" a voice answered. "I need you to call up everyone in the crew Vin. I need an emergency meeting. Tell them all to meet me at the spot behind Geno's Steaks."

"Is everything Ok boss?" "Yeah, everything is fine, just have everyone there in an hour," Mr. Falcone said before he ended the call. With his loaded 9mm tucked under his shirt, Mr. Falcone got into his car and drove away. With anger boiling, he was determined to find out who the rat was.

Chapter 47
Southwest Philly

On the corner of 54th & Chester Avenue, Ski and his cousin Gucci were parked inside a car talking. They had just come back from North Philly looking for Gotti and Marvin.

"That bitch ass nigga can't hide forever," Gucci said, loading up the AK-47. "We will run up on his ass soon," Ski replied. "You know what Ski?" Gucci said. "Wassup?" "Ain't that nigga Troy funeral coming up in a few days?"

"Yeah, why wassup?" Ski asked with a curious look on his face. "Well don't Gotti go with the nigga Troy's sister?"

"Yeah, so what?" "Won't he show some respect and be there to comfort his girl?" Ski sat back in deep thought.

"You might be right Gucci. That nigga Gotti and his sidekick Marvin will definitely be at Troy's funeral. And so will we. We gonna light that motherfucker up and show all these niggas that we ain't playing. Fuck them all." Ski said.

"No, kill them all," Gucci laughed as he finished loading his AK-47.

Atlanta

"Okay, I'm on it. Love you and be safe," Coolie said into his cell phone, before ending the call. "Who was that?" Meeka asked with a look of jealousy.

"Calm down baby girl, that was my cousin back in Philly. She needs me to do something for her, now come back over here and get back in bed." Meeka dropped her silk robe and stood there displaying her perfect, dark hourglass figure. The sight of her body had Coolie at a full erection.

"We have to take a lil' trip soon," Coolie said. "Well right now I'm going to take your sexy ass on a trip around the world," Meeka said, as she got on the bed and slowly climbed on top of Coolie's naked body. "I'm about to fuck you so good Daddy!" she said, as she straddled his hard dick and placed it into the deepest part of her pink paradise.

Fox Street Mall

Roy Carter was a man of many secrets, too many. He was known as a stand-up man, determined to help take all the criminals from off the streets. He was one of the few men that Federal Prosecutor James Hightower trusted. But there was a dark side to Roy Carter as well. For two years he had been secretly paid by King, the boss of the Philly drug world, supplying King with vital information on informants, drug raids, and so much more. His greed for money overrode his loyalty to the Federal Government. Because of his disloyalty, a bunch of government informants had been murdered

Seeing the Black Mercedes parked inside the Shoprite parking lot he slowly approached the passenger side window. When the tinted window rolled down, Roy passed King a small, white envelope. King then passed him a small yellow envelope with $10,000 cash inside. No words were spoken as the window went up and the car slowly drove away. Then Roy placed the envelope inside his jacket pocket and calmly walked away.

~~~

Inside his lavish Wynnewood, PA townhouse Gotti and his girlfriend Tori were lying in bed talking about all the events that had happened. "I'm really sorry about what happened to your brother and that your father closed down the club."

With tears rolling down her face Tori said, "Thanks, babe. But it will be okay, my father is a strong man, and I'm learning just to accept the painful reality of losing my brother. I just want whoever's responsible to pay for what they did!"

"They will, I promise you," Gotti said, placing his arms around her shoulders. "Are you coming to the funeral?"

"Yes babe, I will be there to support you and your pops," Gotti said as he placed a kiss on Tori's cheek. "I love you, Daddy. I'm the luckiest woman in the world to have a man like you in my life, "she tearfully said.

Chapter 48
South Philadelphia

Inside a small row home behind the famous Geno's Steaks, Mr. Falcone, his right-hand man Vinny and three other Italian men were all seated inside. Everyone could plainly see that something serious was on Mr. Falcone's mind. Fear rested in each man's heart. Suddenly Mr. Falcone stood up from the table and pulled out a loaded 9mm pistol and said, "Everyone except Vinny go stand on the wall."

"Hey, what's going on?" one of the men said. "Just get on the fucking wall!" he ordered. The three men all did as they were told. "Go check these motherfuckers for wires Vin."

Vinny walked over to the men and started searching each man one by one. "They all clean boss," Vinny said after he was done. Mr. Falcone nodded his head and told the men to all relax. Then without any hesitation, he pointed his gun at Vinny and shot him twice in the head. Everyone stood there watching as Vinny's lifeless body slumped hard to the floor.

"Check his body Tommy," he told one of the men. Tommy rushed over to Vinny's corpse and started checking under his shirt. Seconds later, he pulled out a small wire and tape recorder that was taped to his stomach.

"Damn, Vinny was a rat," Tommy said in a surprised voice. "How did you know?" he asked. "I knew someone in my crew was ratting. After he checked all of youse and found nothing, I knew it had to be him. Youse guys are the only people I discuss business with."

The three men were all speechless with confused looks on their faces. "Get rid of this rat and destroy that wire. I'm leaving town fellas. Tommy, you are in charge now. I will keep in touch and continue to run things from a distance. Be careful out here and trust no one. As youse guys can see, even your closest friends will turn on you," Mr. Falcone said, before turning and walking out of the room.

Chapter 49
Later that Night
South Philly

When Marvin walked into Jazzmin's house, he noticed her sitting on the couch crying. He closed the door and rushed over and sat beside her. On the small table was a bottle of Grey Goose Vodka and a blunt. Her eyes were bloodshot, and Marvin could plainly see that she had been stressed out over something.

"What's wrong?" "I have something to tell you. It's been eating me alive," Jazzmin sobbed. "Just tell me what it is," Marvin replied. Jazzmin looked into Marvin's eyes and said, "I know who killed Troy." "You do?" he asked.

"Yes, I know who they are. They are the same four men that's been going all over the city robbing drug dealers. Troy was the person behind it all. Troy put them on all the people that came through his father's club."

"How do you know all of this?" Marvin asked. "Me and Joy were helping him. We pointed out certain people that would come in the club, mainly the drug dealers." "Did you have something to do with..." "No, I would never do that. That was Troy and Joy. I quit because they were getting too greedy. I couldn't do it anymore! But they continued on with everything. Plus they were secret lovers."

"Troy was fucking his father's girl?" Marvin asked surprisingly. "Yes, they been fucking for a while."

"So who are the four guys that robbed us?" Marvin asked. Jazzmin took a sip of the Grey Goose and said, "They are four cops from the 16th Police District on Lancaster Avenue. The leader is a guy named Ron. They call him Green Eyes."

Marvin sat back and listened as Jazzmin told him everything she knew. With a treasure trove of information, he rushed out the door.

Chapter 50
1:42 PM
Downtown Philadelphia

Candice Shaw walked up to the crowd of shocked onlookers with a disturbed look on her face. The head of Vincent Costello had been placed on the hood of her car. Besides it was in a Ziplock bag was Victor's cut out tongue and a small note.

Candice stood there speechless and boiling with anger. The people responsible had done this devilish act right outside of her job at the District Attorney's office, and no one saw a thing. Candice walked over and read the note inside the Ziplock bag without touching it. She didn't want to interfere with any clues or fingerprints when the detectives and CSI team arrive.

The Note said:

This is what happens to all rats. Since they won't hold their tongue, you can.

Candice stood there knowing who was responsible. She knew that Vincent Costello was a made mob member and the underboss of the Joseph Falcone crime family in South Philly. They had found out about his cooperation with local and federal authorities, and it had cost him his life.

Candice just turned around and calmly walked away. When she entered her office, she called her friend James Hightower and told him what had just happened. "I want to take him down now!!" she barked.

"Okay, I will get the arrest team on it and we will go get Falcone's ass off the street ASAP! We have information on where he's staying so don't worry Candice when we get him he will never see the streets again!"

Finally, a smile came to Candice's face. After ending the call, she sat down at her desk and began making more calls.

Chapter 51
Laurel Hill Cemetery

On Ridge Avenue, the line of cars followed the black hearse and limousines into the cemetery.
Unbeknownst to all the family and friends one of the cars in the funeral procession had three armed gunmen inside.

Inside a gray Toyota Rav-4, Ski, his crazy cousin Gucci and their friend Tip were waiting for the right opportunity to strike. They had been parked right outside the funeral home, but never got the chance to get a good shot on Gotti or Marvin. Plus there was a police car parked right across the street. That's when Ski decided to follow the procession of cars to the cemetery.

After everyone had parked and got out of their cars a swarm of people crowded around the burial site and listened as the preacher spoke and read a few Bible scriptures. When Ski had spotted Gotti and Marvin he and Tip walked around the opposite side of the cemetery while Gucci hid nearby behind a large tombstone. They were each dressed in all black to blend in with the crowd of mourners.

Standing next to Gotti was his girlfriend, Tori. Right across from them was Big Nook and Joy; she was crying and sobbing uncontrollably. Beside them were Marvin, Jazzmin, and Country. After Ski and his boys had been situated, they took out their weapons and prepared themselves for the inevitable massacre.

But someone else was also out lurking in the shadows. He had been hiding behind a tombstone watching everything that was going on at the crowded cemetery. He had seen Ski, Tip, and Gucci and was suspicious of their presence. With his two .40 caliber handguns loaded he crept towards them.

Chapter 52
Chestnut Hill, PA

A swarm of FBI agents, local police and a twelve man SWAT team surrounded the beautiful two-story home. Candice Shaw was seated inside a patrol car. She didn't want to miss the opportunity to see the man that was responsible for her parents' murders and so much violence and chaos finally taken down. With excitement running all through her blood she watched as the FBI and the SWAT team knocked down the front door and stormed the home.

A few moments later, the agents and SWAT team members walked back out the front door. After a thorough sweep of the home the only person that had been apprehended was a short, heavyset Mexican woman that appeared to be the housekeeper. Candice Shaw rushed out of the patrol car and ran up to the frightened female. "Where is Falcone?!!" she asked.

The woman was scared out of her wits, but still, she said, "Mr. Falcone left a few hours ago," in a Spanish accent. "Where did he say he was going?" Candice asked.

"He said something about a long, Mexican vacation. Then he packed his suitcase and left out. That's all I know, but he did leave a letter on the table."

"What letter?" Candice asked. One of the SWAT members walked up to Candice and handed her a small letter. It said: For Candice.

Candice stepped away from everyone and took the note inside. "One day we will meet again. When we do one of us must fall," the note said.

"Take her away," Candice said, before getting back inside the car. Candice was incensed, angry beyond all words. Joseph Falcone had slipped away once again. But she wouldn't rest until he was dead or in prison.

Chapter 53
Laurel Hill Cemetery

The sound of rapid gunfire started exploding throughout the crowded cemetery. Mourners were running, hiding behind cars and tombstones and falling from gunshots. Ski and Tip were shooting recklessly at the hysterical crowd. On the opposite side, Gucci was shooting his loaded AK-47 like a madman possessed. It was like a scene straight out of a Rambo movie.

Gotti grabbed Tori and hid behind a parked car. He had his gun in his hand but didn't know who was shooting at them and where they were shooting from. Screams and moans of the wounded filled the air. Marvin had also managed to take cover behind a tombstone, but Jazzmin, Big Nook, and Country weren't as successful. The AK-47 bullets had instantly killed them all. Joy had run for cover and hid behind a large tree. She had never been this scared in her entire life.

While Ski and Tip were shooting and focused on killing Gotti and Marvin, the tall, slim man walked up behind them. Without hesitation, he aimed his two .40 caliber pistols at the back of their heads and squeezed the triggers. Pow! Pow! Pow! Pow!

He watched as Ski and Tip's bodies fell to the cold ground. Instantly, life had escaped them. Knowing that they were both dead, he put his guns away and rushed over to Gotti and Tori. Suddenly, all the shooting had ceased, and people were lying on the ground crying, screaming and calling on God.

After Gucci had unloaded the AK, he ran off and disappeared into the back of the cemetery. While running away, he had seen Ski and Tip lying on the ground in pools of blood. When it was finally over five people were dead, and over twenty had been wounded by gunfire.

Chapter 54

"Follow me, Gotti, my car is right over there," Coolie said to Gotti and Tori. They both followed Coolie towards his car. Marvin wasn't too far behind them, but he was holding his left arm as he had been shot. When they approached the car Coolie's girlfriend, Meeka was seated behind the wheel.

After they had been all inside she sped off down the cemetery road and onto the main street. "What are you doing back in Philly?" Gotti asked. "Donna called me a few days ago and told me that some guy named Black was looking for you and you may need my help. So I came down as soon as possible. I was at the funeral, but I didn't come inside. I was just going to watch you and Marvin's back and lay low until I knew y'all were safe," Coolie replied.

Gotti didn't say a word. He just sat there holding his girlfriend, Tori in his arms. She was crying and shaking uncontrollably.

"We gotta get Marvin to a hospital, his arm is bleeding," Coolie said. Meeka followed Coolie's direction as they headed towards the nearest hospital.

"Don't be upset with Donna, she didn't trust these streets, and she only called me to watch your back, "Coolie said. Gotti didn't say a word, but he wasn't upset at all. Coolie had saved his life, and things could have been so much worse. The good thing was that they all left the cemetery before the cops showed up to the gruesome scene.

Moments later, Marvin was getting dropped off at Temple Hospital, while Coolie drove Gotti and Tori back to their Wynnewood home. Once inside Coolie told Gotti everything he saw and about the two men he shot and killed. Gotti still needed answers, and once all the smoke cleared, he was on a mission to find out everything.

Chapter 55
Three Days Later

Down at the 30th Street Amtrak Station, Joy was seated alone on a bench waiting for her train to Miami, Florida to arrive. She had had enough of Philly and all its drama. It was time to move on and start a new life somewhere else, in a warm climate. Inside her suitcase was $100,000 worth of jewelry and $200,000 in cash. Money she had stolen from Big Nook's home safe.

Standing in a small crowd a man had been watching her every move. He was dressed in a black leather trench coat with a black ski mask covering his head. Clutched inside his palm was a 9mm with an attached silencer. The man worked his way through the crowd and approached the bench where Joy was seated. Then he aimed his gun at the back of her head and squeezed the trigger.

In a split second, her lifeless body slumped to the side. Then the man grabbed the briefcase and calmly walked back through the crowd. Back outside he climbed into the waiting Black Range Rover.

"Everything good Gotti?" Coolie had asked before he drove off. "Yup! That no good bitch is right where she belongs. With her good for nothing lover," Gotti replied. "Now let's go get Marvin and take care of the rest of our business.

Gotti had learned that Ski was the man behind the cemetery massacre, but he hadn't been alone. Whoever was shooting the AK-47 had gotten away, because that gun wasn't found near Ski and Tip's dead bodies. He was determined to find out who was the other shooter. But at the moment he, Marvin and Coolie had bigger fish to fry. There were four crooked Philly police officers that needed to feel the wrath of Black Gotti.

Chapter 56
Later that Night

After getting with Roscoe and gathering all the necessary information on the four crooked cops Gotti had learned everything he needed to know for his plan to go smoothly. Roscoe had discovered the four officer's true identities. They were all a part of a special drug task force that specialized in taking down drug dealers.

Once they had linked up with Troy, he told them about all the big time drug dealers that would come to his father's after hour club. They supplied him with GPS tracking devices to place on certain cars so they could follow the intended target's home and rob them for drugs and cash. Gotti had found out what kind of car the cops drove, their work schedules and more. He also found out that the leader of the crew was a man named Ron Bates; A 6 foot tall, muscular black man with fine, curly hair and piercing green eyes. Roscoe had also hacked into the 16th District computer database and found pictures of their undisclosed employees.

~~~
Candice Shaw had her hands full. The media and the press were all over the savage cemetery murders. Five people were dead, and over twenty people were in hospitals suffering from severe wounds. It was one of the worst shootings in Philly's violent history, and it was a total embarrassment for the D.A.

offices. No one had been arrested, and two gunmen were dead at the scene.

The national and local media all wanted some answers. Even the Governor and Mayor were demanding some type of answers. But at the moment Candice had none. So far all she had were five dead people and over twenty wounded with a crazed gunman on the loose. Not to mention that her career was hanging in the balance and she would most likely be facing a suspension and be placed on administrative leave. After all, this black eye was a major hit on the D.A.'s office.

Chapter 57
38th & Lancaster Avenue
West Philadelphia

Jollie's West was one of the most popular bars in West Philly. Crowds of partygoers would be lined up outside just to get in and party, drink or eat with friends. It was also a popular hangout spot for cops, rappers, beautiful women, and drug dealers. Jollie's was located in the middle of one of the most violent neighborhoods in Philly; a section known simply as "The Bottom." Murders, drugs, and robberies were all too common in this rough, West Philly neighborhood.

For the past two hours Gotti, Marvin and Coolie were sitting inside a parked van right outside of Jollie's West. They had planned everything and was now waiting for Ron Bates and his three friends to come out and get into their cars. The moonlit sky was pitched black, and hardly anyone was outside on this cold, winter night.

Suddenly the four men all staggered out of the bar. Each of them was half drunk and unaware of their surroundings. Inside they had been partying up a storm, spending wads of cash, drinking and flirting with beautiful women. Gotti, Marvin, and Coolie got out of the van holding guns with silencers attached. Without any hesitation, they approached the four drunken cops and started unloading their weapons into each of them except Ron Bates.

Ron Bates just watched as his three friends dropped like flies to the cold ground. He froze when Gotti pointed the gun at his head and said, "Go ahead and try to be a hero and you will die right where you stand."

Scared and half-drunk he watched as Marvin and Coolie stood over his friends and finished gunning them down in cold blood. Gotti grabbed Ron Bates and pushed him towards the parked van. When Marvin and Coolie both got inside Coolie sped off down the dark empty street. Ron Bates sat back impaired and confused. Everything had happened too fast to react, and now Ron was sitting in the back of a van with a loaded gun aimed at his forehead.

Gotti looked into his green eyes and smiled. Then he looked down at his sneakers and said, "I see you're still wearing the same Jordan's that you robbed me in." "Do you know that I'm a cop?" he drunkenly slurred. "You won't get away with...this...I will...hunt all you...motherfuckers...down!"

"You're a crook Ron, and you fucked up and robbed the wrong nigga," Gotti said. Moments later, the stolen van pulled up and parked across the street from Doc's house. Gotti and Marvin shoved Ron out of the van and walked him toward Doc's house.

"Take this van somewhere and torch it," Gotti told Coolie. They watched as Coolie drove away. Once Ron was inside he was taken down to the basement where Doc was patiently waiting for his arrival. As they tied Ron to a large table, Doc couldn't help but notice his piercing green eyes. "Amazing!" he said, staring into Ron's eyes.

"Who the fuck is this weirdo?" Ron said. Doc walked up to Ron and put his mouth to his ear. "Your worst nightmare! And I can't stand cops," he whispered. "Fuck all youse freaks! I will have y'alls head for all this," Ron said.

Doc reached into a drawer and took out two sharp, 12 inch knives. "No sir, I'm going to have your head," he said before he started detaching Ron's head from his body. Gotti and Marvin stood back and watched as Doc cut off Ron's head. Afterward they watched as Doc removed Ron's green eyes from their sockets. The scene was gruesome, but Gotti and Marvin stood back and watched Doc in his psychopathic element.

"Don't worry about his body my homeless friend and I will enjoy every bit of it. I haven't eaten a cop in a few years," Doc said with a devilish smile. Doc placed the set of green eyes inside a small Ziplock bag and tossed it over to Gotti. "This is what you asked for, right?" "Right Doc," Gotti replied.

Gotti put the bag inside his jacket pocket before he and Marvin walked up the basement stairs and out the front door. Parked out front inside of a Black Range Rover Coolie had been patiently waiting for them. When they both got inside Coolie slowly pulled off down the street.

Right outside of the Jollie's West bar a large crowd of shocked police officers and partygoers were standing around the three dead bodies. Ironically no one heard or saw a thing. The lights from police cars and ambulances were flashing all over the street. A line of yellow caution tape secured the area, while detectives searched for any clues that would help them solve the triple homicide of these Philadelphia police officers.

At the same time, a massive search had taken place to find Officer Ron Bates, whose body had yet to be found. ABC, CBS, NBC, and KYW news vans were parked nearby, and reporters were running around trying to get interviews and get footage of the crime scene. With three dead officers and a missing cop, the Philadelphia newspapers were going to have a field day. After the three bodies had been bagged and taken to the morgue, the stunned crowd began to disperse.

Chapter 58
One Week Later
Genoa, Italy

Joseph Falcone sat in his chair smoking his favorite Cuban cigar. He had purchased a small villa not too far from the Liguria Sea. The sixth largest city in Italy, Genoa was the perfect place to escape from the long arm of the law. The local police had all been paid off to notify Mr. Falcone if anyone came asking about him. Mr. Falcone had let his hair and beard grow out to change his appearance. He had gained an additional fifteen pounds and had plastic surgery to alter his facial appearance. With over three million dollars stashed safely away in a Cayman Islands bank, Mr. Falcone was set for a very long time.

Still, a part of him couldn't get Philly off his mind. It was his birthplace and home for over fifty years. Plus he had a major score to settle with his arch rival Candice Shaw. He made a promise to himself to one day return home to Philly and send Candice Shaw with her dead parents. But today he sat back enjoying the sun and the cool breeze.

As he sat back smoking and blowing a cloud of smoke from his cigar a beautiful, tall female walked out of the villa and approached him. "Va tutto bene?" she asked.

"Yes, I'm fine," Mr. Falcone answered. He watched as the woman turned and walked away. Then he took out his cell phone and called a number.

"Wassup old man?" Gotti answered. "Thanks for everything. If it wasn't for you, I would be serving a life sentence in Lewisburg Penitentiary."

"It's all good. You just be safe and stay out of trouble old man." "Don't worry; I will. You do the same," Mr. Falcone said. He ended the call within sixty seconds so it couldn't be traced by authorities.

Chapter 59
Delmonico's Steakhouse
City Line Avenue

The Hilton Hotel on City Line Avenue was one of the most lavish hotels in all of Philadelphia. Large glass doors, paintings, and a grand piano filled the lavish lobby. Sitting at a table in the back of the restaurant were Gotti, Marvin, Biggie, and King.

"I came across some info that I think can help y'all," King said before he sipped on a glass of red wine. Gotti and Marvin were all ears. "I found out who the other shooter at the cemetery was."

"Who is it?" Marvin curiously asked. "His name is Gucci, and he can be a major thorn in our side," King replied.

"Yeah, we have known about Gucci for a while. He's reckless, and the nigga is fearless, plus he's the leader of a small gang of hoodlums called B.O.D.," Biggie said. "What is B.O.D.?" Gotti asked.

"Blood or death," King answered. "He was Ski's older cousin. He had just come home from prison, and his choice of weapon is the AK-47."

Gotti and Marvin listened as King told them everything he had known about Gucci and the B.O.D. "How do y'all know so much about this dude?" Gotti asked. King took a deep breath and said, "He used to be a street lieutenant in our organization a few years back. That was until he stole four kilos and $70,000 then disappeared. Like I said, Gucci is reckless and fearless. We have been looking for him for years, but now that his cousin is dead he will come out of hiding."

Gotti took a sip of his wine and said, "Don't worry, Gucci will get the same thing that his cousin got, a bullet to the back of his head."

With a serious expression, King looked at both Gotti and Marvin and said, "This is not a game fellas, unlike his cousin Ski, Gucci don't play checkers, he plays chess. We have to get him before he gets us."

22nd & Lehigh Avenue, North Philly

Inside a three-story home, Gucci and a few members of his B.O.D. crew were all seated inside the living room. Two AK-47s and three 9mm handguns were lying on a table. There were also four bulletproof vests and enough ammo to supply a SWAT team. Gucci stood up showing off his brown 6 foot 3-inch muscular physique. A small tattoo of B.O.D. was near his right eye, and three teardrop tattoos were beneath his left eye. He had been violent nearly all of his life.

It all started at age 12 after he had stabbed his stepfather to death because he beat up his mother. Since then there was no looking back. The only person he had ever trusted and loved was his cousin Ski. But since his brutal death at the cemetery things hadn't been the same for him. He had become more violent and hardened.

"That nigga Gotti is a dead man! Him and all his crew! They killed Ski and now everyone they love has to die for my loss!"

"What about King and Biggie?" one of the guys said. "They are major players in the city," he added.

Gucci gave the guy a hard stare and said, "Fuck em all, it's war!!" Everyone started smiling and nodding their heads in agreement.

"B.O.D!" Gucci shouted. "B.O.D.!! B.O.D.!! B.O.D.!!" the group of men began chanting. "Blood or Death!!!" Gucci yelled out.

Check out this exclusive insert from Black Gotti 2

1:26 A.M
Three Months Later
Wayne & Chelten Avenue
Germantown

    Inside of the black Mercedes Benz, Gotti and Marvin were talking while riding through Wendy's drive-through. Earlier that day, Gotti had met with his lawyer downtown and paid the requested fee so he could represent one of his men who had caught a drug charge. As they waited by the drive-through window for their food, Gotti noticed a short, stocky, dark-skinned man slowly creeping up on the passenger side door. Gotti quickly grabbed his loaded .40 caliber, and without hesitation, he opened the passenger door and started firing his weapon at the man. The man was struck the times in the chest, and Gotti watched him as he clutched his chest before falling to the cold, hard, ground.

    As Gotti jumped back into the car, Marvin sped away into the darkness of the night. Suddenly, a silver Ford Taurus appeared and followed them down Chelten Avenue. With one man at the wheel, two others hung out of the windows and began firing at Gotti's car. Marvin sped up and made a sharp left turn onto Greene

Street, and then he went down one ways, drove on the sidewalk, and cut through a gas stations before managing to get away from them. The attempted hit had happened so quickly, but thankfully, they both managed to get away unscathed.

Gotti instructed Marvin to pull over and park the car. The car was a target, and they needed to ditch it, so they got out and called for a ride.

"We gotta do something about this shit! That's the second time in a week one of those B.O.D. niggaz tried to run up on us!" Gotti vented. "I already have the crew on it! We have to get Gucci. Once we knock the head off, the body will fall," Marvin said before they got into their awaiting ride.

About The Author

Jimmy DaSaint, was born and raised on the hard, gritty streets of West Philadelphia. By his early teenage years, he was running the streets, selling drugs and getting arrested for petty crimes. In the early 90's he started a neighborhood rap group called I.C.H. (Inner City Hustlers). The group quickly became one of the most popular rap camps in Philly. But early 1995, four I.C.H. members were brutally murdered inside a small row home near 42nd & Mantua Avenue.

A few years later, in 1997, Jimmy was shot ten times during an attempted kidnapping. He was comatose and would awake one month later. Still recovering but always a hustler, he continued to grind. In 1999, two of DaSaint's I.C.H. artists (Oschino & Sparks) received a major recording deal with Jay Z's Roc-A-Fella label. Shortly after his artists were signed, Jimmy was set up by a close friend; who was an FBI informant. After being indicted on multiple drug charges, Jimmy was arrested and sentenced to ten years in Federal prison.

In early 2000 Jimmy decided that his prison sentence would not be the end of him. He began writing urban novels, and within two years, he had written over ten. Two of which earned a publishing deal from A&B book distributor in New York. Making him the first federal inmate to achieve such a feat.

After his release in 2009, Jimmy started his company, DaSaint Entertainment. His enterprise is responsible for some of the biggest concerts, music, magazine issues, artists and events in Philly. And though he always keeps his eyes open for all opportunities, he continues to keep his pen close. With over thirty novels under his belt, Jimmy DaSaint continues to write with the rawest passion and fire that you can only get from the streets of Philly.

WE SHIP TO PRISONS

Black Scarface

Black Scarface II

Black Scarface III

Black Scarface IV

DOC

King

Contract Killer

Killadelphia

On Everything I Love

Money Desires & Regrets

What Every Woman Wants

Young Rich & Dangerous

The Underworld

A Rose Among Thorns

A Rose Among Thorns 2

Sex Slave

WE SHIP TO PRISONS

Black Gotti

Ain't No Sunshine   WHO?   The Darkest Corner   Hottest Summer Ever

Place Your Order Now & Thank You For Your Continued Support!
Jimmy DaSaint

COMING SOON

KING II   Black Gotti 2   The Crew   The Rise of A Dynasty

DASAINT ENTERTAINMENT ORDER FORM

Please visit www.dasaintentertainment.com to place online orders.

You can also fill out this form and send it to:

DASAINT ENTERTAINMENT
PO BOX 97
BALA CYNWYD, PA 19004

TITLE	PRICE	QTY
BLACK SCARFACE	$15.00	_____
BLACK SCARFACE II	$15.00	_____
BLACK SCARFACE III	$15.00	_____
BLACK SCARFACE IV	$15.00	_____
DOC	$15.00	_____
KING	$15.00	_____
CONTRACT KILLER	$15.00	_____
KILLADELPHIA	$15.00	_____
ON EVERYTHING I LOVE	$15.00	_____
MONEY DESIRES & REGRETS	$15.00	_____
WHAT EVERY WOMAN WANTS	$15.00	_____
YOUNG RICH & DANGEROUS	$15.00	_____
THE UNDERWORLD	$15.00	_____
A ROSE AMONG THORNS	$15.00	_____
A ROSE AMONG THORNS II	$15.00	_____
SEX SLAVE	$15.00	_____
AIN'T NO SUNSHINE	$15.00	_____
WHO	$15.00	_____
THE DARKEST CORNER	$15.00	_____
HOTTEST SUMMER EVER	$15.00	_____
BLACK GOTTI	$15.00	_____

Make Checks or Money Orders payable to:
DASAINT ENTERTAINMENT

NAME: _____

ADDRESS: _____

_____

CITY: _____ STATE: _____ ZIP: _____

PHONE: _____

PRISON ID NUMBER _____

$3.50 per item for Shipping and Handling
($4.95 per item for Expedited Shipping)

DASAINT ENTERTAINMENT ORDER FORM

Please visit www.dasaintentertainment.com to place online orders.

You can also fill out this form and send it to:

DASAINT ENTERTAINMENT
PO BOX 97
BALA CYNWYD, PA 19004

TITLE	PRICE	QTY
BLACK SCARFACE	$15.00	_____
BLACK SCARFACE II	$15.00	_____
BLACK SCARFACE III	$15.00	_____
BLACK SCARFACE IV	$15.00	_____
DOC	$15.00	_____
KING	$15.00	_____
CONTRACT KILLER	$15.00	_____
KILLADELPHIA	$15.00	_____
ON EVERYTHING I LOVE	$15.00	_____
MONEY DESIRES & REGRETS	$15.00	_____
WHAT EVERY WOMAN WANTS	$15.00	_____
YOUNG RICH & DANGEROUS	$15.00	_____
THE UNDERWORLD	$15.00	_____
A ROSE AMONG THORNS	$15.00	_____
A ROSE AMONG THORNS II	$15.00	_____
SEX SLAVE	$15.00	_____
AIN'T NO SUNSHINE	$15.00	_____
WHO	$15.00	_____
THE DARKEST CORNER	$15.00	_____
HOTTEST SUMMER EVER	$15.00	_____
BLACK GOTTI	$15.00	_____

Make Checks or Money Orders payable to:
DASAINT ENTERTAINMENT

NAME: _____

ADDRESS: _____

_____

CITY: _____ STATE: _____ ZIP: _____

PHONE: _____

PRISON ID NUMBER_____

$3.50 per item for Shipping and Handling
($4.95 per item for Expedited Shipping)

PO BOX 97
BALA CYNWYD, PA 19004
WWW.DASAINTENTERTAINMENT.COM

WANTED: AUTHORS

Authors if you are interested in a potential Publishing Contract with DaSaint Entertainment, please be sure to read this carefully.

Submit a synopsis of your work, along with the first four chapters of your book, and a reading submission fee of fifty dollars to:
DaSaint Entertainment, PO Box 97, Bala Cynwyd PA 19004. No submissions will be accepted without the required fees. Money orders only-made out to: DaSaint Entertainment. **Send copies because your material will not be returned!**

Due to the volume of entries, you will be contacted within six months of your postmarked submissions. Should your entry be chosen, you will be given further instructions and will become a part of the DaSaint Entertainment Family.

Note:
- All work must be the author's original material. No plagiarized works will be accepted!
- You can not be under contract with any other publishing house, and the work you submit must not have been published before.
- DaSaint Entertainment reserves the right to refuse any works based on their professional evaluation.

We look forward to reviewing your work!
DaSaint Entertainment

FREEPORT MEMORIAL LIBRARY

FREEPORT MEMORIAL LIBRARY

Made in the USA
Middletown, DE
22 June 2017